Mike Faricy
Ting-A-Ling

Published by Credit River Publishing 2014

Copyright Mike Faricy 2014

All rights reserved. No part of this publication may be reproduced, stored in a retrieval system, or transmitted, in any form or by any means, electronic, mechanical, photocopying, recording or otherwise, without the prior and express permission of the copyright owner.

All characters in this book are fictitious, and any resemblance to actual persons, living or dead, is purely coincidental.

Copyright 2014 by Mike Faricy

Ting-A-Ling

ISBN-13:978-1505300093

ISBN-10:1505300096

Acknowledgments

I would like to thank the following people for their help & support:

Special thanks to Dan, Donna, Rhonda, Julie and Roy for their hard work, cheerful patience and positive feedback. I would like to thank family and friends for their encouragement and unqualified support. Special thanks to Maggie, Jed, Schatz, Pat, Av, Emily and Pat, for not rolling their eyes, at least when I was there. Most of all, to my wife Teresa, whose belief, support and inspiration has, from day one, never waned.

To Teresa

"Listen here mister..."

Ting-A-Ling

Chapter One

My phone rang out in the dark, *ting-a-ling, ting-a-ling*. The sound indicated an unknown number and I debated answering as I came awake.

"Hello, hello." I cleared my throat a couple of times and looked over at the digital clock glowing on top of my dresser. It was after two in the morning.

"Oooh, is this Den?" A woman giggled. I couldn't place her sexy voice, but I guessed from the slurred speech she wasn't feeling much pain.

"Actually, it's Dev, Dev Haskell. I'm wondering if maybe you might have the wrong number."

I heard what sounded like a distant toilet flushing before she said, "I don't think so, honey, is this…" She repeated my phone number back to me sounding an awful lot like she was reading it.

I glanced over at Heidi lying next to me in a 'two bottles of Prosecco' induced sleep. She was breathing deeply and wore a contented smile on her face. "Yeah, that's my number. What can I do for you?"

"That sort of depends, you tell me. It says here to call if I'm looking for a good time."

5

"What?"

"Right here on the door, it…"

"The door?"

"Yeah, in the ladies room. Someone wrote your number on the stall door. Well, unless you snuck in here."

"Ladies room?"

I suddenly heard a loud *whoosh.* "Yeah, I'm down here at Bunnies. I'm in the middle stall," she said as if that explanation would somehow clear things up. "Your number is right below the hook to hang your coat on. There, all finished. Anyway, I'm calling for a good time. Believe me I could use it right about now."

"Actually, much as I'd like to help you out, I'm wondering if I could get a rain check. I'm sort of in a meeting right now."

"Oh yeah, figures, someone called ahead of me, right? My whole night has gone that way. The guy I was with ditched me about ten-thirty, stuck me with the bar tab and left me here. They had last call about fifteen minutes ago, now I gotta grab a taxi home. Oh well, you can't blame a girl for trying."

"Yeah, unfortunate timing. How 'bout I give you a ring tomorrow?"

"I'm not sure I'll remember."

"I will. Okay if I call you?"

"I suppose."

"What's your name?"

"Danielle, but everybody calls me Danielle."

I waited for a punch line, but there didn't seem to be one coming. I heard a squeak that was most likely the stall door opening. "Well, I better get going, it's gonna take forever to catch a taxi."

"Thanks for the call, sorry I can't help. I'll talk to you tomorrow, Danielle."

"Promise?"

"Yeah, I promise."

"You won't forget?"

"I won't."

I set my phone back on the dresser. Heidi's heavy breathing was beginning to grow dangerously close to a snore. I figured if I woke her there was a chance it could lead to better things and she was probably still Prosecco'd enough not to remember in the morning. I shook her shoulder gently. She rolled halfway over on her back and gave a little sort of grunt. I moved back under the covers, snuggled up against her and lightly ran my hand along her side a few times. Each time I roamed just a little further down until my hand began its final approach launching off her hip bone. She rolled over and just as I was thinking 'success' she rocketed back with a quick, sharp elbow that caught me on the cheek bone. I saw stars, literally and had to shake my head a few times to get my bearings.

Heidi returned to her regular deep breathing.

Once my head cleared I decided to leave 'well enough' alone. Just to play it safe I took an extra pillow and placed it between us.

It was early morning. The sun was up and I guessed it was sometime before seven. I was vaguely aware of Heidi climbing out of bed and walking down the hall into the bathroom. I drifted back to sleep. Maybe ten minutes later I heard the shower running. Sometime after that she walked into the bedroom. I sort of half opened my eyes, hoping she might climb back in bed. I rolled over thinking I could lend some encouragement.

She had her thick white bath towel wrapped tightly around her and my bath towel wrapped around her hair.

She wore a surprised look on her face that suggested something like I had two heads. She stopped and stared.

"What?" I said.

"What the hell happened to you?"

"Huh?"

"What do you mean, huh? That black eye, dopey. You walk into a door or something in the middle of the night?"

"Black eye?" I sat up and turned to face the mirror over my dresser. It looked like I'd stepped in the ring with someone a lot faster than me. My left eye and cheek were swollen and purple.

"Oh, God. Thanks for this."

"Me?"

"Yeah, I just tried to pull the blanket over your shoulder last night because you seemed to be cold and you gave me the elbow. I guess no good deed goes unpunished."

"I didn't do that. Did I?"

I nodded.

"Really? I couldn't have," she said then tenderly felt her elbow.

"Yeah, and that's about all the action I got."

She stared at me for a moment, then said, "Oh, so that's it. The sympathy vote. You probably did that just to talk me into climbing on…"

"Yeah, Heidi, that's right, I beat myself up so you'd feel sorry and crawl back in bed with me," I said, then waited. I counted silently, wondering if it might just work. I could see the wheels turning inside her head. I made it to nine before she spoke.

"You know, you're so stupid, Dev. But that's kind of sweet, in your own warped little way. Oh, God, I really shouldn't, I'm just out of the shower."

"I don't mind."

"Amazingly, I wasn't thinking about you."

"I was just hoping it might relieve some pressure. God, I think I've got a headache coming on." I gently touched my swollen cheekbone.

"Okay, okay, but make it fast," she said and dropped the towels.

Chapter Two

When we finished Heidi lingered just long enough to drink the last of my coffee and eat the one remaining blueberry muffin I had saved for myself.

"Actually, I was gonna eat that muffin."

"Too bad, you should have thought about that when you made me stay and work up an appetite."

"I didn't tell you, you had to stay. I was merely thinking that after I picked up the tab for dinner last night, your two bottles of Prosecco, and the after dinner drinks you couldn't seem to live without, that maybe you felt guilty about falling asleep on me. I certainly put in the time."

"Guilty? No, not really."

"Well, you should."

"Sorry. Not. Look, I had a great time and then I was tired from a really long day. Did I tell you I closed that Buchner deal?"

"Yeah, at least a half dozen times and by the way, you weren't tired from an exhausting day at work. It was the two bottles of Prosecco, *'your best'*, if I recall your order correctly. And then those after dinner drinks. What was it?"

"Did I order a dessert Manhattan?" She sounded like she really couldn't recall.

"No. You ordered two of them. You sure needed those."

Heidi shrugged.

"No doubt you remember the ride home."

Her blank look said otherwise.

"I had to keep pushing you off. You were crazy, wanted me to pull over so we could *'make impetuous love'*…was how you phrased it. I think."

"Oh, sorry about that. Maybe I did have a little sip too many."

"Yeah, followed by that second bottle of Prosecco and then..."

"Okay, okay. Look I gotta run, I've got a luncheon meeting. Hey, if you find my thong, it's red, hang onto it for me. I couldn't find it, unless you did something typically stupid and crude, you perv."

"Actually, I think it's down on West Seventh, right near the stoplight at Grand Ave."

"What?"

"Yeah, you said you felt imprisoned or something along those lines and you threw it out the window. I can't remember exactly. It was just before your *'impetuous love'* suggestion."

"Are you kidding me? Damn it, that was about an eighteen dollar thong."

"There you go, I'm always telling you not to wear one in the first place. See what happens when you ignore my common sense suggestions."

She shook her head and said, "You really are a perv. See you later, I gotta run." She scooped up her purse and the rest of my blueberry muffin and ran out the door.

"Thanks, Heidi."

"My pleasure." She waved over her shoulder, but never bothered to look back hurrying to her car in the cold weather.

I had my phone out as she pulled away from the curb. No rush, I ended up leaving a message. "Hi, Danielle, this is Dev Haskell. We spoke last night, actually this morning, early. Just calling back. You can reach me at this number. Thanks."

Chapter Three

I showered and took my time getting into the office. It was close to noon before I was able to stare out the window at The Spot bar and ignore the files on my desk. I was supposed to be doing some fact checking on job applications for an insurance company. The work was boring, but it paid the bills, at least for this week. I just had to make phone calls and verify periods of employment, some references, nothing too heavy. I figured I could put off making the calls for a few more hours and still complete everything by about four in the afternoon. I planned to call late enough so I wouldn't get an appointment with my pal Eddie Bendix until tomorrow at the earliest.

Eddie was an old high school buddy and the HR guy at a major insurance company. I think they were gearing up to handle the influx they expected from Obamacare, although things were so screwed up on the government end no one seemed to be in a hurry.

It was winter, or would be officially in a couple of days. We'd already had ice and snow for three weeks and temperatures had hung below freezing since Thanksgiving. The day was cold and gray and seemed to match my mood. Oh, and we were out of coffee in the office.

I was staring out the window when Louie came in the door. We shared the office. Louie was fast becoming the man to talk to in town if you got nailed on a DUI, a driving under the influence charge. I think a combination of his personal experience, along with a pretty sharp legal mind were beginning to serve him well. The personal experience wasn't the sort garnered in the court room. Louie had been pulled over enough times, and never yet been charged making him a bit of a legend, at least with the liquid diet crowd.

"I think you were doing that the last time I saw you," he said, then threw his briefcase on the picnic table that served as his desk. He discarded a grimy ski jacket on top of the briefcase and tossed his Minnesota Wild stocking cap on top of the jacket, it fell on the floor where he ignored it. All of his suits seemed to be permanently wrinkled. He was in the same wrinkled gray suit he'd worn the previous two days.

I sort of came back to the present and stopped staring out the window long enough to answer him.

"Just thinking. I'm not at all excited about checking out those employment applications for Eddie." I indicated the two untouched stacks of files on my desk.

"What the hell happened to your eye? And you haven't done those yet? The files…you've had them for at least a week."

"Actually, I just got them last Monday."

"Yeah. And today is Friday. That's a week. Right?"

"I was thinking seven days, you know, not five. Anyway, I'm not all that excited about making the calls. Most of the time I'm lucky if they'll even confirm

14

employment, let alone the dates. These companies are always worried about being sued by some jack-ass lawyer and don't want to say much of anything beyond 'hello'."

"Tell me about it. And the eye?"

"Nothing really, just grabbed some dinner last night with Heidi. She sort of bumped into me with her elbow. It was an accident. Hey, get this I got a call in the middle of the night from some chick. She was reading my phone number off a stall door in the ladies room."

"The ladies room? Okay, I'm ignoring your Heidi explanation for the moment. You wrote your phone number in the ladies room?"

"I wasn't the one who..." My phone rang and I answered.

"Haskell Investigations."

There was a momentary pause before a voice said, "Hello, I'm returning a call left for me from a Mr. Haskell?"

"That's me." I recognized her voice from last night and nodded at Louie. "Is this Danielle?"

"Yes." Her response suggested our conversation wasn't going much further.

"I'm returning your call from last night. Actually, it was early this morning, just after two," I explained.

"My call?"

"Yeah."

"I've had a lot going on lately and I'm wondering if you might have me mixed up with someone else." She was suddenly sounding just a little unsure.

"You phoned me from the ladies room. I think you said the middle stall. Apparently my phone number was written on the door and you called."

15

There was a long pause and I had the sense the event was slowly coming into focus. "Oh, God. Look, I apologize. I'm really sorry I bothered you. It won't happen again, I promise. I may have had a little too much to drink and I..."

"I think you said some guy ditched you and you got stuck with the bar tab. Hopefully you found a taxi home."

"Yeah, I did. Not my boyfriend, by the way. But back up for a minute, you're an investigator?"

"Yeah, Haskell Investigations."

"So, what do you investigate? Is it like in the movies and on TV?"

"Usually it's a lot more boring." I glanced over at the stacks of untouched files on my desk.

"Do you ever take on new clients?"

"On occasion. It sort of depends on what they want me to do. Sometimes they would be better served by an attorney or the police."

"You ever investigate cheating partners and that sort of thing?"

"You mean like a husband or boyfriend?"

"Not really, I was thinking more along the lines of a business partner."

"I have."

"Really, gee, maybe we should talk." She made it sound like I had just passed some sort of test.

"Do you want to set up a time when we could meet?"

"All right." She suddenly sounded guarded. "Maybe a public place where we would both feel comfortable."

I took that to mean where *she* would feel comfortable. "You pick the place," I said.

"How about the St. Paul Grill? Could you maybe do tomorrow, say about sixish?"

"I could. I'll plan to see you tomorrow about six. I'll be seated at the bar."

"How will I know you?"

"I'll be wearing a brown bomber jacket, I've got dark hair combed back and right now I've got a black eye."

"A black eye," she said, but didn't comment further. "Okay, I'll see you tomorrow, about six, at the bar."

"Right," I said, but she'd already hung up.

Chapter Four

It was way past six and getting closer to seven. I was headed toward the bottom of my second beer. It was standing room only at the bar and I must have been the only person in the place not attending a Christmas party. Everyone was dressed to the nines in silk Christmas ties or long fur coats and talking about five octaves too loud. Between my blue jeans, bomber jacket and the black eye I stuck out like a sore thumb.

"Excuse me, do you work here?" She was an attractive brunette, with a chest fighting to escape the confines of her dress. I had to concentrate to focus on her face.

"No, sorry, I'm actually waiting to meet someone. She's running a little late." I didn't see any point in mentioning the close to an hour part.

"Are you Dev?"

I think I blinked or half jumped. "Danielle?"

She nodded and held out her hand. "Danielle Roxbury, nice to meet you." The extended hand gave me the opportunity to glance down her dress. Yeah, they were really trying to jump out and get some air.

"Sorry I'm so late, my car wouldn't start. I think it's that stupid battery again and I...excuse me, Dev, up here. Hello."

"What? Oh sorry, I have a hearing impairment. Service related." I took a sip of my beer and let that seep in.

She looked like she wasn't buying it and had probably heard something along that line a few thousand times. She studied me a long moment before she spoke. "Actually, I'm really running late. I'm on my way to somewhere else, another get together, you know the Holidays. I had to taxi down here. God, I feel like I've been running late all day."

"Look, we're not going to be able to talk, let alone hear one another in this place. I could give you a ride and we can talk on the way. It'll save you a taxi fare."

She seemed to consider my offer for a moment before she finally nodded. "Okay, I guess." She sounded less than enthusiastic.

Some fat guy with a red face and an empty martini glass began to ooze onto my bar stool before I was even off the thing. We made our way through the crowd and were almost out the door when she stopped.

"Hold on, I just want to make a call and let them know I'm on the way," she said. Her cell was already up against her ear. "Hey, Karen. Yeah, I know stupid battery again. Anyway, a guy is giving me a lift." She looked at me and nodded. "I'll be there in fifteen. Dev Haskell. Yeah, I tell you later. Can't wait, see you shortly. Okay, yeah, bye."

I wasn't sure there had even been someone on the other end of the line, but I couldn't blame her for playing it safe. "I'm parked just around the corner. You want to wait here and I'll pick you up? It's pretty cold."

"Oh that's sweet," she said and looked surprised.

19

I didn't waste any time walking to my car. It was damn cold and I hoped the heat would begin to kick in by the time I drove around the block. There was a parking ticket frozen onto the windshield of my Lincoln Continental. Merry Christmas from the city of St. Paul and the parking Gestapo. I fired up the engine, tossed the box holding Eddie's files into the back seat, then made a half hearted attempt to scrape the frost off the inside of the windshield. I had the heater set on defrost and blowing cold air full blast. It didn't seem to be helping. I thought of running the wipers until I remembered I was out of washer fluid. By the time I drove around the block I think it had actually gotten colder in the car.

I pulled into the circular entry and stopped opposite the door. A valet with a questioning look on his face bounced out the door. I lowered the passenger window. "Just picking up."

"Good luck, man." He gave my car a quick once-over, chuckled and bounced back inside.

I think he said something to Danielle standing there with her hands in her coat pocket because she gave a sort of disgusted grimace when she looked out the window. She took her time then seemed to grit her teeth and stepped out into the cold, taking quick, tiny steps toward my car. I had to reach over and open the passenger door because the handle was broken on that side. The door was frozen closed and I had to pound on it a few times before it creaked open.

"Hop in."

"You sure?" she said then cautiously climbed in. She stayed as close to the passenger door as possible. She thrust her hands deeper into her pockets, then pulled her coat around her like it was a hazmat suit and she might contract some incurable disease from the

20

interior of my car. Her chin was buried about four inches beneath the collar. Just her eyes peeked out.

"Heat's just about to kick in," I lied. "Where to?"

"Up the hill to Summit Ave., about two blocks this side of Dale. Do you know how to get there?"

"Yeah," I said, pulling onto the street. "I live up there."

"You live on Summit?" she asked, sounding incredulous. It was the toniest street in St. Paul and she didn't bother to hide her surprise.

"No, but close, just a couple of blocks away."

"Oh," she said then followed up with, "Brrr-rrrr."

I drove down West Seventh to Grand Ave and turned right. Fortunately, we didn't have to wait at the stop light.

"Oh, God, how old is this thing? Is your heat on?"

"It's a classic and I think the heat's getting ready to start. So, you said you needed some investigative work done?"

"Mmm-mmm, God. It's so cold." Her shoulders looked to be up around the top of her ears and her voice came out muffled from somewhere deep within her heavy coat.

"Would you care to expand on that?"

"God, I'm freezing to death. Are you sure the heat is on? I can't feel my toes."

"Almost. What did you want me to look into?"

"Oh, God, I can't stop shivering."

"We'll be at your party in about three minutes. I think you'll survive." I felt the vague hint of warm air beginning to bounce off the windshield. As we approached Ramsey Hill the light turned yellow and I stepped on the gas. It turned red about the time I reached the intersection, then sailed through. The hill was extremely steep, so I gave the accelerator another push about halfway up the hill. The Lincoln sputtered then coughed a couple of times before it sprang back to life.

"Oh, God no, please," Danielle whined to herself from somewhere deep down in her coat.

"We were discussing your investigation."

"Huh? I was thinking of having you check out a guy who owes me a lot of money."

"The guy who left you stranded the other night?"

She grunted a noncommittal response.

"Why does he owe you money? I mean, did he just take it, drain your bank account or use your credit cards?"

"No, nothing like that. Matter a fact he's a banker, or at least he was. He's a lawyer too now that I think about it. I lent him some money for his business."

"Which is?"

"His business? He's into all sorts of rubs and barbecue sauces and things. He went commercial last spring. He has an industrial kitchen, somewhere. He's developed packaging, that sort of thing. He's moving the stuff into stores, the farmer's market, some trade shows."

"Is it any good?"

"I don't know. To tell you the truth I never tasted it. I'm a vegan."

"A vegan who invested in barbecue sauce…interesting."

"That's it, up there on the left. The brick house with the white trim and dark shutters. See, where all the candles are. Oh, God, brrr-rrrr."

The place was a large, three-story, brick colonial with a double front door centered on a long porch with lots of pillars. There were maybe a dozen large, round ice globes on either side of the front sidewalk with candles burning inside that illuminated the way. It looked pretty upscale and although I'd been past the house a million times I'd never been inside.

"Let me just turn around here so you don't have to cross the street. It's slippery and you're in heels."

"That would be nice," she said, sounding unconvinced.

"I'll walk you to the door," I said thinking I could at least scam some free drinks and who knew where that might lead.

"No thanks," she replied in a tone that suggested no further discussion.

"Look, Danielle, I might be interested in the investigation. Why don't you call me and we can chat some more." Then I made the u-turn and pulled ahead so she could exit the Lincoln, step out onto the candle lit sidewalk and another world.

"Here's my card," I said and handed it to her.

She kept her hands buried in her pockets and her shoulders raised close to the top of her head. I held my card out there for a very long moment before she reluctantly snatched it and thrust her hand back into her coat pocket.

"Give me a call if I can help," I said.

"Yeah, look, thanks for the ride. I'd ask you in, but well, you probably wouldn't know anyone. Better get that heater looked at," she said then shouldered the door open. She quickly got out, turned and ran as fast as she could in heels toward the front door.

Nothing like a first impression. I leaned over and pulled the door closed then headed down to The Spot for my own brand of Christmas cheer.

Chapter Five

It was the following Tuesday. I had blanked out my 'meeting' with Danielle about sixty seconds after she fled the scene. I just remember the heat suddenly came on in the Lincoln before she'd even made it up to that ritzy front porch and I took that as an omen.

I'd been sitting in my desk chair looking out the window at a cold, gray, empty street for the better part of the morning. Occasionally someone would hurry into The Spot, but with the temperature hovering right around arctic for the past few weeks people were so bundled up I couldn't recognize anyone. At this rate it would be months before there were any women on the street worth leering at.

My cell interrupted any otherwise unproductive day.

"Haskell Investigations."

"Dev?"

"Yes."

"It's Danielle," she said, sounding like I should be excited to hear her voice.

"Hi, Danielle." I tried to hide my disappointment.

"I'm calling to discuss your employ," she said, then proceeded to rattle off a laundry list of names,

24

addresses, phone numbers and suspicions. Basically, it boiled down to Danielle lending a guy named Renee Paris fifty-grand about a year ago. She wanted it back and he suddenly didn't seem interested in talking to her. Aside from the fact that his name sounded like something out of a 1960's movie I didn't think she had a leg to stand on.

I actually knew the guy, or rather, I knew *of* him. Usually when someone talks about what a rat a particular person is there's a good chance a listener might just chime in with, *'Yeah, but he's got a sick kid, the business is going bad or there's been a death in the family,'* in an effort to explain away pain-in-the-ass behavior.

No one ever countered in that manner when the name Renee Paris popped up. They usually listened to the tale of abusive chicanery and then countered with, *'You think that's bad, you should hear what that bastard did to us.'*

Renee Paris is what's politely referred to as a *developer.* I'm sure there are some very good people who fall into that category. In the case of Renee Paris, he's also a jerk, a cheat, a liar, short of stature and a self-absorbed asshole with a long history of dubious business and real estate undertakings.

If the cops ever found him sitting behind the wheel of his car with a bullet between the eyes, they'd have to rent the Xcel Center just to hold all the suspects.

That said, it still seemed no matter how bad his reputation, he was always able to find the next person to fleece. I figured Danielle was just the latest victim in a long line of victims.

Well, and of course, there was one more thing about Renee Paris. I had a childhood acquaintance, Jimmy White, not a pal anymore, but only because I hadn't seen him since we were in high school. Jimmy died a few years back. He'd apparently gotten involved with Renee Paris in some sweetheart sort of real estate deal.

After Jimmy filed for bankruptcy, lost his business, lost his home, and then his reputation, he felt he had nothing else left to lose and so he took his life. I didn't know a lot of the facts and I'm sure it was more complicated than one jerk pushing Jimmy over the edge, but I wasn't a fan of Renee Paris right out of the starting gate.

"And Danielle, I'm guessing you don't have any sort of signed agreement, letter of intent, stock options, anything like that. Correct?" I asked.

"Well, yes, I guess technically that's correct. But, he knew I wanted to be paid back. I told him as much when I gave him the money and he promised me he was good for it."

"The fifty-grand. Was that in the form of a cashiers check?"

"Actually, he said that cash would work better."

"Of course," I said.

"He said he'd pay me back just as soon as he could."

"But cash?"

"He said it would be better for tax purposes, you know, not having to report it and all. I don't know much about that sort of thing and well, Renee does. He knows all that technical tax sort of stuff."

"You got anything in writing, maybe a phone message or a text that attests to the fact you loaned him money?"

"Not really. Renee thought it would be more personal, you know if we looked one another in the eye

26

and shook hands. *'My word is my bond,'* he always said."

"How's that working?"

"Not all that well, I guess."

"I'm not exactly sure how I'll be able to help. Frankly, Danielle, it sounds like you may be better served hiring some junkyard dog attorney who could go after him in a court of law. About all I could do in an investigation would be to tell you where he's having dinner and maybe who he's with."

"From what I know of him, if he actually had an inkling that I hired a private investigator and he was being followed, I think that might go a long way in getting him to respond to my requests. He can get kind of paranoid."

"Paranoid? Like he could go crazy? I don't want to push him into doing something violent." I didn't add *'toward me'*.

We spoke for another minute or two. She passed on Paris' address and phone number to me. None of our conversation seemed to point to a very successful undertaking, but then again it was two-fifty a day plus expenses.

"Okay, Danielle, terms are four days in advance to put me on retainer. Plus expenses, I verify all expenses with receipts. I don't mark up expenses, I just past the cost along to you. And just so I understand, you want to know where he goes and who he's with. I'll report that to you what, daily, weekly?"

"Daily would be good."

"Okay, I'll begin just as soon as you get that retainer to me."

"Give me your office address and I'll have it to you within the hour."

She did get it to me, although it was more like three hours, and in cash, ten crisp hundred dollar bills. I wrote out a receipt for her, but she just waved it off saying, "I trust you, Dev."

I tossed her receipt in my desk drawer.

Chapter Six

The first thing I did was call my contact down at the DMV.

"Department of Motor Vehicles, how may I direct your call, please?"

"Donna, extension four-one-three."

"One moment, please."

"DMV, this is Donna."

"Hi, Donna, Dev Haskell."

There wasn't so much a long pause as it was just dead silence. I finally blinked. "Donna? Hello?"

"What do you want?" she whispered, then sighed as if to suggest she couldn't believe her bad luck.

"Just need a little information on someone."

"I've told you before, you can't continue to do this. I've just been moved up a civil service grade level and your call is putting all of that at risk."

"Guess you should have thought about that before you started luring underage interns into your bed. Not so sure the state HR department will look too kindly on that sort of activity, or your husband for that matter. I don't know, what do you think?"

"I'm not discussing this any further." Her whisper ended with a hiss.

29

"Good, because I need any information you have on someone named Renee Paris."

"The developer? Is he the one who stuck the city with that empty department store?"

"Among other things. I'm guessing he's aged middle to late forties. Violations, date of birth, prior addressees, anything you can find." I spelled out his name and gave her the address Danielle had given me. "There can't be too many guys in your files with that name."

"This sort of thing is going to take some time. Don't call me."

"You've got my number?"

"Unfortunately," she said and hung up.

I didn't hear from Donna until the following morning. Maybe not so amazingly I was busy doing the same thing, basically nothing. I was sitting in my office chair staring out the window at a cold, gray, empty street. I'd counted two people scurrying into The Spot in the past hour and a half.

"Haskell Investigations."

"I've got that information for you. You're going to need a pen and some paper."

"Who is this?" I joked then spun the office chair around. The only thing that had moved on my desk in the last few days was my coffee mug. I picked up the pen I'd pocketed at the liquor store. There was a blank yellow legal pad on the desk and I sort of brushed my hand across it to remove some of the dust and doughnut crumbs.

"Do you want this information or not?"

"Yes, Donna, sorry, just closing the file I was working on. Okay, let me have it." There was another one of her long pauses, but I could sense her mind

30

working. I'm sure she was envisioning a variety of ways she would like to *'let me have it'*.

"Renee Paris, the address you provided is the same one we have on record. DOB twelve August, 1968. Two moving violations, one a minor speeding charge, sixty-nine in a fifty-five, that was in 2005. An accident in 2011, he was found at fault, speeding, no proof of insurance, license suspension for ninety days before reinstatement. That's standard. I found four prior addresses, the first in 1987…" She read off his previous addresses, mentioned he was listed as an organ donor on his driver's license and gave me his height at five feet four inches and his weight, one hundred and eighty-five pounds. Short and kind of stocky.

"Can you email me his license photo."

"No."

"What do you mean no?"

"I don't want any sort of trail suggesting I've ever had contact with you."

It was my turn not to say anything. I waited for close to a minute before she finally spoke.

"Give me your address and I'll mail it to you, but this is the last time. I really mean it. You've certainly gotten more than your pound of flesh from me. Honestly." She wasn't yelling, but she was close to it. Judging from the background noise I guessed she'd found one of the few remaining pay phones in town and had called me on that. I gave her my office address.

"Is there anything else?"

"No, Donna. I appreciate…" She hung up before I could finish.

I looked over the notes I'd taken. At least from the stand point of the DMV Renee Paris looked like your basic upstanding citizen. I knew better and went online to search his business activity.

31

Chapter Seven

LuSifer's Treats. It took me a moment to put it together. Renee Paris was either a lousy speller or too clever by half. LuSifer, a take off on Lucifer, I guessed. Being a former banker and lawyer turned real estate developer I thought the whole devil aspect was more than a little appropriate. It appeared that based on some moderate success at regional fairs and food competitions Renee had put together a business selling sauces, rubs and about a hundred different articles of clothing. The site sold everything from aprons, to T-shirts, to little red-satin devil's horns and, of course, his Bar-B-Que sauces. Amazing how far a borrowed fifty-grand in cash could take you. His online store was just that, online, so no physical address was available. I decided to take a drive past his home address and check it out. I figured he was probably working the online business out of his house.

The address on his driver's license had Renee Paris' home located in the neighborhood surrounding a 1913 water tower referred to locally as the Witches Hat tower. The area of hundred-year-old homes is roughly triangular in shape and bounded by the interstate, the Mississippi river and busy, commercial University Ave.

Many of the homes now serve as rental properties for college students, which leads to a constant coming and going. That fact made the address I was checking on stand out all the more.

I spotted the property almost a block away, although I didn't know it at the time. The front sidewalk was unshoveled and judging from all the snow on the six steps leading up to the front yard the place hadn't been entered for at least the past month. It looked like shopping circulars had been stuffed in the mail box until it overflowed. Then they were attached to the front door knob with rubber bands and left to suffer the elements. A number of city inspection notices were attached to the front door and the front picture window.

I was familiar with the notices. Nowadays everyone in town was familiar with them. They were red, blue or white. Basically, they declared the property vacant, the utilities disconnected and the place unfit for habitation. They also threatened a pretty serious fine if you attempted to remove the notices or to enter the property. If Renee Paris owned this place he certainly hadn't been here for a while.

The heat was coming on in my car, finally, and I couldn't see any advantage to trudging around the place through the snow. I tried to phone the number for Paris that Danielle had given me, but the recording said the phone number was no longer in service. I drove back to the office to do what I should have done to begin with, check the county tax records.

Six minutes after sitting down at my desk I knew the property was listed as a category three nuisance. Basically, that meant there had been enough citizen complaints that the city tagged the structure. The place couldn't be sold unless it was brought up to code, and unless it was brought up to code in one hundred and twenty days it could be slated for demolition. Interestingly enough the taxes had been paid through June of next year.

It had always struck me as a short-sighted city policy, but even a city our size had something like twelve thousand abandoned buildings on its hands after the Great Recession. Not the best setting in which to make long range municipal plans. I wondered if the beautiful, but flakey Danielle was aware of the place being abandoned.

"Unfit for human habitation? Really? You're kidding? He just had a new kitchen put in a year or two ago, cherry-wood cabinets, granite counter tops, a special refrigerator just for wine. I'm partial to Pavo, that sparkling white from Portugal. Are you familiar with it?"

She asked the question like she already knew the answer.

"When were you there last, Danielle?"

"His house?"

'No Portugal,' I thought. "Yeah, his house."

"Pretty recently, we had a Bar-B-Que with some potential investors out in the backyard."

"Well if it was out in the backyard, it had to be more than a couple of months ago."

"Let's see, it was either Memorial Day or Labor Day weekend, I always get them mixed up. It was the one with all the flags."

I immediately thought *'Fourth of July'*, then said, "Labor Day is in the fall, first weekend in September."

"September? No, that wasn't it. Only because I was in Tuscany then, with some girlfriends. God, it must have been last spring already. Gee, go figure. Who knew?"

"Danielle, when was the last time you saw him?"

"God, I've tried to put it out of my mind."

"Did you have a disagreement?"

"I'll say, he caused a scene and then told the bartender I was paying the tab before he stomped out the door."

"Well his business still seems to be alive and kicking, at least online. That sort of suggests he could still be in town. Any idea where he would go? Maybe someone he might move in with?"

"No. God, I can't imagine anyone who would want to put up with him, at least not for very long. How long did you say the house has been vacant, a month?"

"That's just what I could determine from no footprints in the snow and the sidewalks unshoveled. I think it has to be closer to six months before the city would act, post the notices the way they did."

"Huh?"

"How often did you see him?" It seemed the logical question. I was beginning to think Danielle had maybe been just a bankroll with benefits for old Renee.

"Well, probably about two or three times a week. He was always over here and we'd maybe go out for dinner or something. I don't like to cook. We'd usually do Saturday night, Sunday. He'd call on Monday, I guess Wednesday nights too. See he always liked to play trivia down at Spanky's, so we had to go there."

"Do you have any other phone number? I called the one you gave me, but it was disconnected."

"Yeah, that seemed to happen a lot. Problems with his phone. He was always getting a new phone with a different number."

"Define a lot. How often did he have a new phone?"

"It seemed like just about every month. He seemed to have the worst luck with service providers."

I was thinking he probably used throw away phones. Buy a cheap phone, pay for a certain amount of minutes and toss the thing when you used them up, virtually untraceable. That might make sense if he was a hit-man for the mob, but a guy who makes Bar-B-Que sauce, it didn't seem to add up.

"And you haven't been in his home since last spring?"

"I guess not. To tell you the truth, I like mine a lot better. It's just a lot nicer and well, my cleaning lady is in here twice a week. I have the sheets changed regularly, the bathroom is clean, and there's always toilet paper. I always have something besides ice cream and a box of cheap wine in my refrigerator."

I'd heard the same sort of comments from a number of my former companions and decided to move on. "I'll see what I can find out about his kitchen, where his sauces and things are being made. But it's beginning to look like he's gone underground and maybe he's been that way for awhile."

"Okay," she said. I waited, but she didn't offer anything else. She was either completely oblivious or what I'd told her wasn't at all surprising. I couldn't tell which it was.

It took some time, but I located his kitchen. It might have been easier had I been trying to locate a meth lab. I came across a number of dormant internet sites, a couple of blogs with postings from four years back and some stale pages on Facebook. I couldn't find any phone numbers or addresses. I ended up doing what I should have done in the beginning. I called a local grocery store chain and lied.

"Yeah, I'm wondering if you can help me. I'm trying to get in touch with the people at LuSifer's Treats. I'm with the paper and I'd like to do an article on them, but I can't seem to get a location or a current phone number."

"The Bar-B-Que sauce people, right? Gee, we've had a lot of success with that particular line."

Right there the woman in purchasing seemed to know more than Danielle.

"That's why I wanted to write an article about them, I'd list your stores as a source, if you don't mind. We wanted to run the article in this weekend's food variety section. You know, get the word out to people right before the holidays."

"Let me just check here," she said. I could hear keys clicking on a keyboard in the background. "Oh yes, here you go. This number should work. If I recall you may have to leave a message, but they seem to be fairly prompt in returning the call. I'm afraid the only address I have here is a PO Box."

I wrote the phone number down, told her thanks, and then got off the line before she wanted any real information from me. At least the phone number was still live. I left a message when I phoned LuSifer Treats and used the line about writing an article for the paper, then sat back and waited.

Chapter Eight

I was still waiting later that night in The Spot. I had drifted in around five-thirty for just one and found out it was Jameson night. That had been a good four hours ago. Bob Seger was blaring on the juke box so loudly I didn't hear my phone ring, but I could feel the vibration in my pocket so I dashed into the men's room to escape *'Old Time Rock & Roll'*. The noise level was a little better, but just barely.

"Haskell Investigations."

There was a long pause before a deep voice said, "Damn it. Wrong number. This God damned phone…"

"Is this LuSifer Treats?" I guessed.

"Yeah." The voice sounded cautious.

"Sorry, I was just joking. I thought you were a pal calling me back. I phoned earlier regarding an article I wanted to write about your line of sauces and rubs. We're going to run it in the Food Variety section, this weekend. We have a lot of requests for product like yours coming up before the holidays and we wanted to get the word out."

"What do you…" The door suddenly opened and one of the regulars half staggered into a stall. Bob Seger

38

filled the small room and I had trouble hearing his response.

"Actually, I'm really unable to talk just now," I said as the door closed. "I wonder if we might set a time and I could meet you for a brief interview, see your facility, that sort of thing."

"What's your name, again?"

"Haskell, Devlin Haskell. I freelance for a number of food publications and trade journals. I'm actually on the beat right now, doing a taste test. I could meet you sometime tomorrow if that would work. You just name the time and I'll adjust my schedule."

"Tomorrow?"

"Yeah, I know it's sort of short notice, but we just had half a page open up. Look, if you can't, no problem, I'll just go on to the next name on my list. Like I said, we wanted to get this in before the holidays. You know how people stock up," I said, then held my breath and waited.

"I can probably do three tomorrow afternoon, but I can only give you a few minutes," he said grudgingly. He made it sound like he would be doing me a big favor and it suddenly felt like I was pulling teeth. If I'd been a real reporter I probably would have told the guy to shove it right about now. But, since I was a phony I said, "Terrific. Where are you located?"

"You know Casey's?"

I thought for a long moment. "The only Casey's I know is a place on Fort Road. I think it closed about a year ago."

"Actually, closer to two years. That's where we're at, we rent the kitchen. It's all legal," he quickly added as an after thought, making me think maybe it wasn't quite squeaky clean. At this point the door opened again

39

and even though it was the men's room, Lady Gaga filled the place.

"I put a finger in my ear and said, "See you at three tomorrow." Then I crossed my fingers and asked, "And your name, sir?"

He waited a moment before he answered, like he was weighing his options. "Paris. Renee Paris," he said and paused for effect. He said his name in a way that made you think applause should follow. Instead the toilet flushed behind me.

"When you get here pull in back. Just ring the buzzer next to the door marked 'Employees Only'. See you tomorrow, three o'clock," he said and hung up.

I left The Spot about fifteen minutes before closing. What I thought was a parking ticket on my windshield turned out to be a plain white, number ten business envelope stuck under my windshield wiper. Nothing was written on the outside. Inside was a printed copy of Renee Paris' driver's license with not so much as a rude comment penned anywhere. I walked around my car just to make sure Donna hadn't slit one of my tires then I drove home.

Chapter Nine

I phoned Danielle first thing the next morning, a little after eleven. I got the impression I woke her.

"Hello?" It was her voice all right, but a couple of octaves lower than normal. I visualized her in a darkened room with the shades drawn. The only thing she would be wearing was a black silk mask that covered her eyes. Skimpy little items of personal clothing probably marked a trail down the hallway to her bed and even though she answered the phone her wrists would somehow be tied to the bed posts with silk cords that…

"Hello, hello?"

"Oh, hi, Danielle, Dev Haskell. Sorry, I was lost in thought. I wanted to give you a report. I'm meeting your friend, Mr. Paris this afternoon."

"Renee? Really? Where?"

"Kind of strange. There used to be a bar, Casey's down on Fort Road. It's been closed for quite a while."

"I know the place, Renee owns it."

"He owns it?"

"Well, he did, the building, that is. Another one of his investments that didn't quite work out. I forget what he was supposed to do, some kind of code violation that

41

was going to be too expensive to fix. Update the sprinkler system or elevators or something. He ignored the citations and the city eventually closed it until the code violations were taken care of. Renee was in the middle of an ongoing argument with the guy who actually owned the restaurant located there. Then he was killed in a car accident and they never reopened the place."

"It sounds like that's the kitchen he's been using for his sauces. I wonder if it's even up to code?"

"That sort of thing never seems to bother Renee."

"Well, I guess we'll soon find out. I'm going to be meeting him there this afternoon."

"He agreed to meet with you?"

"Yeah. Well, I told him I was with the newspaper and we wanted to do an article on his business, the Bar-B-Que sauces. He seemed to buy it."

"And what are you going to say to him?"

"I'm not sure, maybe pretend to be a reporter for a bit, but eventually I was planning to tell him I was hired to investigate him. That you want your money back or at the very least a repayment plan."

"I don't know. I don't think he'll agree to that."

"Probably not. But then again, he doesn't have to agree to anything. I'm just the messenger on this. And, it's a good start for you. I'm thinking if he's halfway serious about his sauce business he can't hide for too long. If he disappears I'll find him again, maybe threaten a lawsuit. I office with an attorney…"

"He's probably threatened like that a couple of times every day."

"Maybe, but at some point he'll have to begin to pay you back, hopefully."

"You should just shoot him or something," she said, then quickly added, "I suppose I shouldn't even joke like that."

"No, you shouldn't. But I understand how you feel," I said.

"Let me know what he says, but I don't think its going to be positive. Like I said he can get kind of paranoid."

"I guess we won't know until I meet with him."

"You'll call me after you talk with him?"

"Yes, Danielle, I will."

Chapter Ten

I pulled into the back parking lot of Casey's a few minutes before three. The windows on all four sides of the building were whitewashed so you couldn't see in. As I drove around the building I noticed someone had smashed all the glass tubes on the neon *'CASEY'S'* sign above the entrance. With the exception of a set of tire tracks leading to the silver Mercedes parked at the back door the half acre parking lot didn't have so much as a footprint spoiling the pristine snow cover. There wasn't a cloud in the sky and although the sun was glaring off the snow, the temperature remained a balmy minus three on the Fahrenheit scale.

I followed the tire tracks up to the backdoor and pulled alongside the Mercedes. I think I could have fit two of the Mercedes in the trunk of my Lincoln. I climbed out and placed my hand on the sleek silver hood next to me. It was cold and had to have been sitting there for at least an hour. There was a short trail of foot prints leading to the back door marked *'Employee's Entrance'*. A shovel rested against the brick building and the concrete pad in front of the door looked to have been recently shoveled. Someone named Peaches had spray painted his name across the buff

44

colored brick. Amazingly no one had bothered to steal the security camera mounted above the door.

I pushed the buzzer and waited. I heard what sounded like distant banging from inside, then footsteps approaching from the other side of the door.

"Who is it?" a deep voice growled from behind the metal door.

"Dev Haskell. I've got a three o'clock appointment with Renee Paris."

There seemed to be the murmur of brief conversation coming from the other side of the door, but when it opened there was only one person standing there. I adjusted my gaze downward. Renee Paris looked a good deal shorter and a lot uglier than his driver's license had indicated, which was a real accomplishment.

He looked me up and down, then stuck his head outside and looked around, I guess to make sure I was alone. "Humpf," he mumbled, then glanced around again before he closed the door behind me. The hallway was dark with the exception of some light oozing out a doorway maybe twenty feet away. Paris headed off in that direction while I attempted to let my eyes adjust from the bright outside. "You coming?" he called over his shoulder just before he walked through the lit doorway.

I hurried to catch up and entered an industrial kitchen area. There were at least half a dozen, large aluminum caldrons sitting on a massive stove over low burners. Each caldron was partially covered by a flat, metal lid slid halfway across the top. The caldrons looked to hold about five gallons and something was slowly bubbling in each one. You could just make out the sound of a soft boil, like a distant brook rippling.

The scent was rich, almost tangy and my mouth began to immediately water.

A large metal table, maybe ten feet long stood alongside the stove and was littered with cooking debris. Onion skins, garlic skins, empty spice containers, a couple empty flats that had apparently held tomatoes and empty packages of butter and brown sugar were scattered all over. Large, sharp chef's knives with black handles and white plastic cutting boards lay amidst the mess.

Opposite the stove was a long aluminum sink with water running out of the tap and a cloud of steam rising up off a stack of industrial sized frying pans. The sink gurgled and there was a half filled bucket beneath it on the floor catching a steady drip from the drain.

"So?" Paris said accusingly, like I was already wasting his time. He leaned back against the metal table, folded his arms across his chest and sized me up. Apparently charm wasn't his strong suit.

"Mr. Paris."

He gave a single cold nod, like a cop or a pissed off school principal. I felt like I was standing before him having to ask forgiveness for somehow being foolish and growing taller than he was.

"Mind if I call you Renee?"

He shrugged, then said, "Whatever," sounding like he really couldn't be bothered. His attitude rankled me. A faded image of my childhood pal, Jimmy White popped into my head and I could feel my temper begin to rise. My face flushed slightly and I wanted to brace the little bastard up against the table, slap a pair of handcuffs on him and then stab him in his fat butt with one of those sharp knives.

Instead, I smiled sweetly and asked, "What can you tell me about your sauce?"

Paris sort of shrugged and shook his head like he couldn't believe I was that stupid. Then he said, "Get screwed, you prick. We both know why you're here and it hasn't got one God damned thing to do with a newspaper article. You got a message to deliver, do it, quit wasting my time and then get the hell out."

"Okay, fair enough," I said and cut to the chase. "Danielle wants her fifty-grand back. Or, at the very least some sort of payment plan."

"Payment plan? I made her the beneficiary on my damn life insurance policy. Anything happens to this place and or any number of my other investments and she's the beneficiary there as well. I'll tell you another thing…"

"I think she's looking for something a little more immediate than thirty or forty years down the road. She lent you some cash with the idea you would pay her back. I think you even used the line, *'You were good for it'* and *'Your word was your bond.'*"

"That's what it always is with your kind, isn't it? You just can't comprehend the intricacies of high finance, it's simply beyond you. What you need to do is take…"

I straightened and held my hand up to cut him off. "Wait a minute, I'm not finished. I know you're a savvy guy. You rub shoulders with the 'swells', the movers and shakers here in town. You got the right people as friends. Let me just give you a word of advice. If you're thinking of not paying her, maybe just lying low or even hiding, it took me about four minutes to find you. Only because my phone call was put on hold for three of those minutes. You may be some hot shot banker with a law degree, but you're swimming in the same toilet with me right now. I'm the nice guy. Next time someone comes around they aren't going to be so nice."

"You're threatening me. Is that it? I should have known. Typical of your kind. Trying to scare me...I suppose you're going to yell some ridiculous profanity next and beat your chest."

"No. I don't threaten. I'm going to warn you right now, if I'm yelling there really isn't a problem. But when I'm speaking softly, like I am now, that's when I'm most dangerous." I could feel my very short fuse suddenly become exposed

"Dangerous?" He half laughed. "You muscle bound clown, where in the hell did she find..."

Boom. In a flash I remembered Jimmy taking the heat on a neighbor's broken window and not telling on me. We were maybe eight or nine. Suddenly, everything seemed to go in slow motion. It always does. Paris was leaning back against the work table with his arms folded, looking smug, calling me names and talking tough. I guess he was just used to being able to insult people for no particular reason. I took a quick step and kicked his feet out from underneath him. As he hit the ground he let off a loud, "Uff!" when he landed on the concrete floor. On the way down the back of his head caught the edge of the table with a dull sort of thunk. There wasn't any blood, at least that I could see. But, he was going to have a hell of bump, maybe even a slight concussion. One could only hope.

His eyes crossed as I grabbed him. I half threw him, half rolled him over facedown, then took his left arm and twisted it up behind his back. I grabbed him by the back of his collar and yanked him to his feet.

"Ahhh, ahhh, ahhh, ahhh," he groaned as I raised him up. I marched him toward the sink and the steaming water, picking up speed with every step. By the time we reached the sink we were moving at a fast

48

paced trot and I slammed him into the edge of the sink and shoved his head under the tap.

It burned my hand which suggested it was even worse running over his thinning hair and down the back of his neck. He struggled to get free and I slammed his head into the faucet a couple of times in an effort to hold him under the stream of scalding water.

"Ahhh, ahhh, God damn it, please, stop, please, please," he screamed from beneath the faucet.

I pulled his head back then released my grip on his arm. As he staggered back his skin appeared scarlet from the water. He might have even gained a blister or two. He fell to his knees, then slowly slouched onto the ground, gasping.

"I'll sue your miserable ass off you son-of-a…"

I reached into the sink, grabbed an aluminum pan and back handed him across the side of his face. The pan made a dull sort of gong noise which I thought sounded rather appropriate.

"Now, see what you made me do, Renee. God, how typical of my classless kind. And, I'm usually such a nice guy. I'm gonna suggest to Danielle, you remember Danielle, you told her you were good for the fifty-grand you borrowed. I'm going to tell her not to take the legal route. I'm going to tell her that won't work with you. I'm going to give her the names of a couple of guys and they're going to come visit you. They won't be as nice as me, Renee. So, if I were you, I'd give Danielle a call and work something out, something a little better than your damn insurance benefits and *'your word as your bond'*. If you haven't called her by this time tomorrow, well, all bets are off. Nice chatting. Don't worry. I'll let myself out. Catch you later," I said. I tossed the frying pan back into the sink and left him there in a steaming puddle on the floor.

Chapter Eleven

"That's what he called you? A muscle bound clown? That's not very nice." Danielle held her wine glass out to be refilled. She sat facing me with her legs curled up beneath her. She seemed oblivious to how very short her little black skirt was and I certainly didn't intend to tell her.

We sat together on an incredibly comfortable leather couch opposite a warm roaring fire. The fireplace was surrounded by an elegantly carved white marble mantle and glazed Victorian tiles. There were real Tiffany stained glass lamps on little antique tables at either end of the couch, and a large oriental rug about two inches thick covered the polished oak floor between us and the fireplace. We were in the library, three of the walls were covered with walnut shelves and lots of leather bound books. Danielle had inherited the home and apparently it came with lots of inherited money.

"I guess he's used to getting his way and intimidating people. Somewhat of a Napoleon complex, I think. You find it from time to time in short males." It might have been the four or five glasses of wine that had me expounding and waxing eloquent.

50

She smiled, looked deep into my eyes and rubbed her hand gently up and down my arm. "I'm just glad you didn't get hurt," she said. She ran her finger back and forth along my shoulder. I tried not to stare too long at her chest as she breathed excitedly. Then I heard what sounded like footsteps above us on the second floor.

"You hear that?" I asked.

"Ghosts." She giggled.

"Sounded more like footsteps."

"Just an old house. Happens every winter, well, and the summer too. Things creak. Glad you're here to keep me safe," she said. Her eyes seemed to flare and the fire crackled. "Do you think he'll call me?" she asked and took another sip.

"I hope so. I really don't know any guys who we could send to threaten him. One guy, maybe, but he's got this really high voice and no, that would be a bad idea right from the get go."

"What if he tries to hurt me? What if he breaks in and comes after me?" she asked.

"I don't believe he's in any condition to do that. Hopefully, you'll get a phone call tomorrow. I don't think you should meet with him, at least not alone. I wouldn't invite him over here. If you do have to meet him maybe bring me along, let him know I intend to be there."

"God, Dev, I don't know. It's so scary. What was I thinking when I loaned him that money?"

"You were just being nice and trusting and it didn't quite work out." I decided not to mention naïve, awfully dumb and clueless.

"Damn it, why does something like this always seem to happen? What if he tries to come here tonight?'

"I don't think he will. He's probably…"

51

"But what if he does, Dev? God, I just don't want to be alone." She was running her finger down my chest - actually all her fingers, sort of scratching me through my sweater.

"You're really frightened?"

She nodded, bit her lower lip and squeezed my hand. I was envisioning her with those silk cords around her wrists. "Well, if you're really frightened, I guess I could maybe stretch out on the couch here. I mean, if you think it would help and make you feel safer."

"I think it would make me feel a lot safer if we were in the same room. In the same bed," she said, then raised her eyebrows and stared at me.

I drained my glass of wine and felt my heart pounding. "Yeah, I can do that for you. That's probably a good idea. You can never…"

"Come on, I've got a bottle of wine open upstairs," she said, cutting me off then she stood and took me by the hand.

Chapter Twelve

If there were little silk cords, I couldn't remember them. I was in a very large bed beneath a very thick down comforter. There was a large, polished wooden headboard with gold carvings along the top rising up toward an ornate ceiling. The corners of the bed had four massive, carved posts with what looked like heavy, red curtains draped along the side and running all the way down to the floor. Each one of the posts had a gold wreath of carved leaves wrapped around the top. The walls of the room had dark wood paneling running up about five feet from the floor and then what looked like red, silky wall paper covering the walls. On the wall above the fireplace a painting of some old, bald guy with a white beard and holding a bunch of papers hung in an ornate gold frame.

My immediate thought was I had woken up in a museum. I couldn't tell what time it was, but there was a razor thin slice of bright light seeping through the edge of the heavy red window curtains.

Danielle lay on her side with her back to me, breathing deeply. She suddenly rolled over and snuggled up against me. "Mmm-mmm so safe," she said.

I felt something solid against my side and reached down. I felt around her waist, and then slowly recalled some of our activity from the night before.

She giggled, snuggled in even closer and whispered in my ear, "Your belt, remember? Ride 'em, cowboy." She gave a little laugh like she was the only one in on the joke. Then she draped her leg over mine and went back to breathing deeply.

I figured it would be impolite to wake or disturb her comfort in any way, so I drifted back to sleep, too.

* * *

Louie was seated at his picnic table desk. Surprisingly, he was reading a file instead of sleeping. It was almost two in the afternoon before I'd made it into the office. I think Danielle felt reasonably safe and very content by the time I left. I seemed to hurt wonderfully, all over, and I was having trouble wiping the smile off my face. I was also minus my belt.

"You look happy," Louie said.

"I've been working a case," I replied and headed toward the coffee pot.

"A case that required lipstick?"

"What?"

"Your neck, on the right side and up on your forehead. She must have been checking to see if you had any brains," Louie said.

"Oh, yeah. See I had…"

"Forget it. Hey, if you empty that pot, make a new one. Okay?" he said and then returned to the file spread out in front of him.

I made a fresh pot of coffee, wiped the lipstick off my face, and asked, "What do know about a guy named Renee Paris?"

54

Louie looked up from his file and gave a loud sigh. His chins shook and he stared at me for a long moment, deep in thought. Then he asked, "The developer guy?"

"Yeah."

"I know enough general information that I'd warn you about any involvement what-so-ever. I think there's a pretty long trail of bodies in his wake. Not that he's killed anyone, but you're never going to come out on the winning end of a deal with him. He's one of those guys who'll tell you that he's sorry you lost everything and you're on the hook for a couple of million, but that wasn't his original intention, so it's just your tough luck. Of course, somehow he always seems to exit unscathed."

"Why would anyone even get involved with the guy?" I was thinking about Jimmy, again.

"Good question. Wishful thinking on their part, I would guess. He travels in a world where a lot of folks believe their own news clippings and they begin to think they're immune from making a mistake. They've probably heard about him, maybe they've even been cautioned, but he holds out some gigantic return on their investment and they can't quite see past that. Besides, he's one of them, nice car, right schools, friends of their friends. Then the rug gets pulled out from underneath them and they find out they don't have a legal leg to stand on. Reality isn't really a strong suit for a lot of those folks."

That seemed to sum up Danielle and her little world.

"Please, don't tell me he's your client," Louie said.

"Yeah, that's right. Do you like his shade of lipstick? Come on give me some credit, Louie. No, it's just a minor deal actually. But, you just described the scenario. A trust-fund beauty lent him money and like you said, now she doesn't have a legal leg to stand on."

"Are you trying to find some angle for her? Because, believe me the guy may be a jerk, actually an absolute asshole. But, he's all about himself and he's not stupid. He always seems to be covered."

"No, I'm not trying to figure out an angle. I just told him she wanted to be paid back or at least have some sort of payment plan set up."

"Let me guess, she did the deal on a handshake?"

"Well, I'd say he probably got a lot more than a handshake." I thought back to my passionate night and then again this morning.

As Louie shook his head his chins sort of waddled from side to side. "I'd say it's probably gone, her money. How much we talking?"

"Fifty-grand."

"That's a lot, but not by Paris' standards." Louie actually sounded surprised. "He's doing deals for multiple millions. Things like selling shares in some incredible retail development where historic buildings used to stand. Building condos that ruin the view for everyone else. Fifty grand sounds like a lot, but it's small potatoes in his world, nothing, just chump change to a weasel like him."

I told Louie about Paris' house, over by the Witches Hat, how it was listed a category three nuisance, unfit for habitation, even though the taxes were paid until next June.

"There's an angle there. I don't know what it is, but there's an angle. Maybe he can take some sort of tax loss on the property for the next five years if the city demo's it. Believe me, he's not the sort of guy to just let that happen. He's working some sort of scam, you can bet your life on it."

"You think my client is in any kind of danger?"

"Your client. You mean the one with the lipstick?"

I nodded.

"No. I mean, not physical, if that's what you're suggesting. But, I doubt she'll ever see her fifty-grand again and I'd maybe change all her passwords and double check access to her bank accounts, that sort of thing. Might want to hop on that right away and get it done as soon as possible."

Chapter Thirteen

I was in The Spot, seated at the far end of the bar. I'd been drinking a couple of Mankato beers and I signaled Mike for another refill. I was trying to wash Jimmy White out of my mind.

"You seem to be kind of quiet tonight," Mike said as he slid my pint back across the bar.

"What can I tell you, Michael? I'm just out there trying to make the world a little better place one good deed at a time."

He shook his head like he didn't believe me, and then moved down the bar for some more enlightening conversation.

I took a sip and glanced up at the TV mounted in the corner. The news was on. I looked at my watch to double check. Amazingly it was already ten. God, I'd just stopped in for one on the way home, go figure.

The news was leading with a local story, fire fighters battling a blaze in freezing temperatures. An arctic vortex they called it. They were interviewing some poor, frost bitten fire chief with icicles hanging from his helmet. The desolate scene was lit by flashing lights coming from the emergency vehicles that gave the whole place a sort of strobe-like effect. The fire trucks, along with all the equipment and the fire fighters were coated with ice. They were still pouring gallons of water onto the rubble of the smoldering building.

I couldn't hear what was being said so I returned to my freshly filled pint and thanked my lucky stars I wasn't out there freezing my ass off. Right around eleven I thought it would be a good idea to drink and dial.

"Give me one for the ditch, Mike," I said and dialed.

"Hello?"

"Hi Heidi, it's the answer to all your dreams."

"Tommy?"

"No, me, Dev."

"God, have you been drinking?"

"No. I'm...well, okay, maybe a couple. Just wondered if you might be interested in some company?"

"No."

"Sure?"

"Yes, very. Look, do you need a ride?"

"That sounds fun."

"No, not that kind of ride, God get your mind out of the gutter. I meant a ride home. I guess I could pick you up if you need it."

With a case of beer under my belt a ride home with Heidi lecturing about personal responsibility and my idiotic behavior didn't seem to be the way I wanted to end the day. "It's okay, sweetie, I'm good to drive. I'll take the back way. Thanks," I said and hung up.

I'd just ordered another beer when someone came up behind me.

"You don't really need that, Dev."

I turned to see who it was. "Heidi?" I wasn't sure at first. Her hair was some sort of recent peroxided

59

blonde thing, almost white. Then she had that little black dot makeup thingy on her face like Marilyn Monroe. Even in my current state, I knew better than to comment on her new hair color. So I figured I would play it safe. "Decide to join me?"

"No. Come on, let's go. Mike, tell sloppy here he doesn't need that beer."

"She just might be right, Dev. You don't need to get pulled over on the way home."

"Yeah, I get it. Okay, I'll maybe just have a Jameson instead and then…"

"No, Dev. Come on, I'll give you a lift if you want it, otherwise I'm going back home and you can just take your chances."

Chapter Fourteen

I woke up facing my bedroom door. It was early enough in the morning to still be dark outside. I couldn't really remember the ride home, but I was pretty sure I hadn't been wearing the black bra that was hanging from the bedroom doorknob.

I rolled over and my first thought was I'd picked up someone's grandmother. Then I hazily remembered Heidi showing up with her new hair color to give me a ride. In the dim light of the bedroom my mind began to gradually replay events until I arrived at my phone call to Heidi. Once again she was a true friend, although I still wasn't sure about the hair color. I guess it was blonde, but in this light it appeared snow white. I knew I'd be asked and so I began to prepare my response.

I walked up the street while she was in the shower, picked up some of her favorite caramel rolls from the bakery and some orange juice. She was on her second roll and eyeing mine. I pulled my plate across the kitchen counter closer to me.

"Okay, you've had time to think about it. So?" she asked.

"I like it," I lied. "I was the luckiest guy in The Spot last night. God, it was like getting a ride home from Marilyn Monroe," I said.

She stared at me for a very long moment, looking like I was out of my mind. "Not my hair, you idiot. God, you're certifiable. No, I mean the conversation we had when I brought you home. The reason I stayed with you last night."

"You needed a reason?"

She gave me a warning look.

"Okay, Jesus, just joking. Let me ask what do you think?" I was at an absolute loss, wondering what in the hell she was talking about and playing for time, hoping she'd say something that would jog my memory.

"Honestly? I think it was really sweet, Dev. In your own sort of Neanderthal way. I just didn't know you had it in you. Imagine, all those years ago and you still remember that little boy not telling on you. What was his name, Joey?"

Bingo. "Jimmy. Jimmy White. Yeah, we were best buds as kids. He was just a lot more driven than me. Well, and smarter, more academic, nicer, kinder, did I mention better looking?"

She shook her head. "You're not getting out of this, buster. Admit it, you actually have a heart."

"Hello. Look, after all I've done for you over the years. We've been…"

"I know why you've done things for me over the years, and it had nothing to do with the heart part of your body." She forced a laugh.

"Maybe sometimes," I said then quickly changed the subject. "Anyway, like I guess I said. I just sort of snapped when this Paris guy gave me the attitude and then there I was, thirty years ago, standing in front of Mr. Graham, the two of us, Jimmy and me. We had our

62

slingshots in our hands, I had the lousy aim and Jimmy didn't give me up. He took the rap and said he did it. I think his folks grounded him for a week and I sort of stayed away for maybe a month. I never had the backbone to fess up."

"Oh, Dev, honey, you were just a little boy. You'd do it now," she said and gave my arm a squeeze.

"I'd have a lot better aim, now. Anyway, I just had a vision of everything going down the drain and Jimmy was the only guy left standing. Jack-ass Paris probably snuck off unscathed and my pal lost everything, his house, his business and all his money. Guess he felt he didn't have anything left or no one cared and he just ended it all. I didn't even know about it until months after. Christ, they found his damn car abandoned in the middle of the High Bridge. Apparently, someone reported he just stopped the car, got out, walked to the rail and jumped."

"Oh, my God."

"Yeah, I don't know if they even found the body. I missed the obit, the wake, the funeral. I'm guessing under the circumstances it would have been a pretty private affair. But I should have been there. I owed him."

"You may not want to hear this, Dev. But, I think you're being a little hard on yourself. When was this, two, three years ago?"

"Two-thousand-seven, actually. You know, in the midst of the financial collapse that we've all recovered from."

Heidi was a very smart money person and a very shrewd deal maker. She didn't respond to my comment.

"I'm sorry I didn't mean it like that. I didn't mean you. You think I should look up his wife? I mean his widowed wife."

63

"I suppose you could. But honestly, what do you expect to accomplish? It may be she blames herself for his death. The circumstances you described, I'm guessing things could still be awfully tough for her. Maybe she thinks it was her fault. She just might like to never, ever be reminded of those days. Did they have any children?"

I looked up at her and shook my head. "Jesus, nice investigator." My voice sort of trembled. "I don't have the slightest idea. To tell you the truth, until the other day, I hadn't thought of any of this for, well, for a very long time."

She slid off her kitchen stool and squeezed my arm. "Don't punish yourself, Dev. That's my job. Come on, you left your car at your office last night. I'll give you a lift back down there." She gave me a lingering kiss on the cheek, then grabbed the rest of my caramel roll, stuffed it into her mouth and went to find her jacket.

Chapter Fifteen

Jimmy White's wife, his widowed wife, was named Susan. As far as I knew she had always gone by Sue. I didn't know if she'd kept White as her last name. I didn't know her address. I didn't even know if she was still in the area. I didn't know anyone I could call to find out. I went online and did a reverse directory search. I came up with thirty-seven different Sue Whites in St. Paul within the proper age range.

I picked up the phone and started calling. I found her on the thirty-third call.

"Sue White, please."

"Speaking," I could hear what sounded like a young voice in the distant background.

"Sue, my name is Dev Haskell. I'm looking for a woman who was once married to a childhood friend of mine, James White."

"Oh, sure, I recognize your name. Yeah, Jimmy mentioned you from time to time. You're what, a fireman, is that right?"

"Actually, I'm a private investigator."

"Really? Is this business or pleasure?"

"Sort of business, nothing you have to worry about. Actually, I was thinking about Jimmy and well, I wondered if I could maybe get together with you."

"You know he passed away a few years ago."

"Yeah, I knew that. Actually, I just wanted to talk to you about some things. I'm involved in an investigation and I just had some questions that..."

"An investigation? About me, about us? God, now what?"

"No, no nothing like that. To be honest, it involves someone who was in the same line of business as Jimmy. I just wanted to see if you could give me some direction. You know, which way to go in this thing. To be honest real estate investment and development is not my strong suit."

She didn't say anything for a moment. "I really don't think I can help you. All that was his world, not mine. I'm an RN, pediatrics. If you have someone who needs a diaper change I might be able to help with that, but real estate and property development is something I don't know anything about and I don't want to know anything about."

"I'd still like to talk."

"I really don't see how I can help," then she seemed to address someone else and said, "Just a minute honey, mommy's on the phone."

"Sounds like you're busy. I promise I'll only take a few minutes of your time."

"I suppose. I've got to pick up at day care so we won't be home until after four-thirty tomorrow."

"If I stopped by around five, could I just have maybe fifteen minutes? I'd gladly pick up dinner."

She sort of laughed and said, "Thanks, but that's not necessary." Then she gave me her address and hung up.

66

Chapter Sixteen

I was in the office by nine the following morning, attempting to learn anything I could about Renee Paris. I started out by Googling his name. Based on the volume of results that popped up I'd be in front of the computer for the better part of the day. I read the first half dozen articles that were posted, three from the *St. Paul Pioneer Press*. A couple more appeared to be a four part series from a local financial publication. There was another long column from the *Minneapolis Star Tribune* that had run in their business section. Those were just the articles in the past few months. Checking dates on the postings, the things went back more than thirty years and there seemed to be a common thread to the headlines. "*Loans Called, Investors Sue, Project put on hold, Code Violation Lawsuit, Court Decision Appealed.*"

I didn't know who was handling his legal maneuvering. Whoever it was, they had to be nicely compensated. While everyone else seemed to end up in the poor house, Paris was still out there walking around free and doing another deal. Meanwhile, the body count of folks who were financially ruined or just couldn't take it anymore continued to rise.

Sixty minutes later, just an hour into my research and pretty much everything Louie had suggested looked to be true. It was sort of like reading about some politician trying to get ahead of an ongoing story. There'd be a statement from Paris attesting to one thing or another and then a story posted a week or a month later, listing all sorts of factual information that read completely contrary to what Paris had said. The common denominator was Paris always seemed to walk away and someone else always seemed to be left holding the bag.

I phoned Danielle in the early afternoon.

"Hi, Danielle."

"Dev?"

"Right, just checking to see if you heard anything from Paris."

"No." The way she said it seemed to suggest something like *'Why would I?'*

"Well, I guess I was just hoping he would respond in some way, a call, an email, something that might suggest he took our little conversation to heart."

"I don't think that's going to happen, Dev. That's not his style."

"There's a word that's not applied to Renee Paris too often, style."

That didn't seem to raise a reaction.

"If you hear anything from him you'll let me know. Right?"

"You'll be the first person I call. Hey, I've got to run, I've got another call coming through," she said.

"Call me back if it's him," I said, but she'd already hung up.

Chapter Seventeen

At exactly five o'clock I rang Sue White's door bell. She lived in a single level, nondescript tract house that looked to have been built in the mid-sixties. Just like all the other nondescript tract homes for blocks around. There seemed to be four or five different versions of the same style. A front door on the right or left corner of the home, a large living room picture window in the middle and what I guessed were two side-by-side bedroom windows on the opposite corner.

The siding on Sue's home was a cedar shake sort of affair with a large flat panel between the picture and bedroom windows painted the same color as the trim. Sue's home was light gray with the flat panel and her trim a peeling white. Her front door was a glossy fire engine red.

I rang the doorbell a second time, hoping she hadn't forgotten. In an effort to try and extract some warmth I moved my hands tighter around the take out pizza box I was holding. The evening temperature was already below zero and dropping. The double cheese and sausage pizza box I held felt barely warm and was quickly losing any semblance of heat.

The door was suddenly opened by an attractive, redheaded woman in hospital scrubs. Her hair was pulled back and wrapped in a loose bun.

"Mr. Haskell?" She smiled.

"Please, call me Dev," I said and sort of raised the barely warm pizza box.

"Come on in. Oh, gee, you didn't have to do that," she said, taking the box. "But, thanks. I was just wondering what I was going to serve Jimmy."

The look on my face must have given me away.

"My five-year-old son. He's at the kitchen counter watching the Grinch."

"Yeah, sure, you had me for a brief moment there," I said, then pushed the door closed behind. I followed her through a living room and into the kitchen. There was a small Christmas tree standing in the corner of the living room sparsely decorated with little twinkling white lights. As I passed I noticed one small gift covered with candy cane Christmas wrap placed beneath the tree.

"Jimmy, this is Mr. Haskell. Would you please look up from the Grinch long enough to say hello?"

He was seated at the kitchen counter and the little face that looked up was the spitting image of his father as I remembered him in about Kindergarten. Close cropped light brown hair, a cowlick hairline and happy blue eyes.

"Hi, Jimmy. Nice to meet you, give me five," I said and held out my hand.

The kid slapped my hand, shot me a quick smile and then made a speedy return to the Grinch.

"Can I get you anything to drink?" Sue asked.

"Are you going to have something?"

"I've got the kettle on for some tea, will that do?"

70

I guessed it would have to. "That would be fine," I said and then tried not to visibly shudder.

"Come on, we can sit out in the living room and talk," she said a minute later. She pushed a steaming mug toward me and walked out to the couch.

I sat down in the threadbare chair across from the couch and put my tea mug on the coffee table. The flimsy little table next to the couch held a twelve dollar lamp burning a ten watt bulb. A framed photo of Sue and Jimmy on their wedding day rested in front of the lamp. She looked gorgeous in a full length wedding gown. Jimmy in a dark suit looked as I remembered him, happy and serious at the same time.

She settled onto the couch, half faced me and folded her legs beneath her. She took a long sip from her mug and seemed to study me. Her hospital scrubs looked to be a faded blue and she wore small white slippers on her feet. "So," she said, setting her mug down. Then she just sat there and waited with a look on her face that said *'your turn'*.

"Yeah, well. Like I mentioned on the phone, I grew up with your husband. I'm sorry, by the way, my condolences. We grew up, grade school pals, sort of started to go in different directions during high school. Jimmy was serious. I think he had something like a three-point-five grade-point average. He was on the track team, student council, wrote for the school paper. I was, well, let me see, I guess I was just me."

She gave me a look like she wasn't quite following.

"I was your typical, confused, goofball at age fifteen."

This seemed to make sense to her and she nodded, then said, "Except neither of us is fifteen anymore."

71

"I probably still am, at least to some extent. Did he ever tell you about the neighbor's broken window?" I asked, figuring she was probably sick to death after hearing about it numerous times.

She shook her head 'no' and reached for her mug.

I told her the story, then finished with, "So anyway, the reason I wanted to talk to you was to learn what I could about Jimmy's dealings. I know he was a developer, that he was involved in real estate investment. I was hoping you could give me an idea of what it was like for him, for the two of you."

"What it was like?" She flashed a smile, a lovely smile. She had smooth soft skin and white teeth that shone almost porcelain, full, sensuous lips, soft brown eyes. "It was somewhere between pure, living hell and the absolute shittiest thing you can imagine."

I must have had a shocked look on my face.

"What? Surprised?" she said. She took another sip of tea, set the mug down and then those soft brown eyes suddenly took on a vicious quality.

"Imagine watching everything you've worked so hard for just going up in flames and then instead of helping put the fire out, your so called partner just seems to pour more and more gasoline on the flames until it's roaring out of control and all you can do is watch. You can't stop it. You can't slow it down. You can't do a thing."

"What happened?"

"What happened?" She let out a long breath and seemed to look into the distance for a moment, weighing her response. Then she refocused and bored back into me with those eyes.

"What happened? I honestly don't know, at least not the specifics. One day we were in a partnership with a man named Renee Paris. Everything is fine, we're sort of half planning the various things we're going to do with our investment returns, a new home, another project, trips, clothes, cars, start a family. The next thing I know we are beyond broke, without a leg to stand on. We lost the condo, lost our lake place. They repossessed our cars. Christ, we even had to sell our damn furniture," she said, then cleared her throat to get her voice back under control.

"Jimmy went to our lawyer. That jerk wanted ten grand, up front before he'd be able to even lift a finger. He came up with it, somehow, the ten grand. Not that it did any good."

"What was his name?"

"The lawyer? God, Richard Hedstrom. He has a small practice specializing in development deals."

"Did he get anywhere? File some sort of court action, an injunction, something, anything?"

She shrugged and gave me a look that suggested 'isn't it obvious?' "It turned out Richard was a pal of Renee Paris. I've always thought they were probably in on the scam together right from the start. No doubt they had a good laugh at our ten grand expense. I think the guy wrote a letter or something, kept telling Jimmy he was waiting for a response, needed another thirty days, that sort of thing. Meanwhile our ship was sinking, fast."

"What happened?"

"We tried to sneak off under the cover of darkness and were followed by a thousand different collection agencies and the IRS. What happened? I can tell you in two words, that bastard named Renee Paris."

It grew very quiet. I heard her swallow. I noticed her face was flushed and her eyes had watered.

"What can you tell me about Renee Paris?"

"Oh, boy." She sighed. "Well, nothing nice. He believes in Renee. At first he's nice, in a smarmy sort of way, but he quickly changes into an arrogant, pushy, lying little son-of-a-bitch."

I nodded. "That seems to be the consensus of opinion around town."

"You don't know the half of it, Dev. Those are his finer qualities."

"Why'd Jimmy ever get involved with the guy? This wasn't the first project Jimmy had done. He was an up-and-coming guy in the business. He'd been around the block a few times. He was going to count in this town. He must have read the press on Paris, known people who ended up on the wrong end of the stick." Now I was getting upset.

"He got greedy. In fairness, we both did. I was more than happy to take the trips, drive the cars, accept the gifts, the jewelry and then one day you wake up knowing there is no possible way you can ever do anything wrong. Because, you're way smarter, luckier and harder working than everyone else. You've got it all figured out. You know all the angles, you're connected. And then..."

I waited for a long moment while she just sort of hung out there, somewhere seven or eight years back.

"And then?"

She shrugged. "Like I said before, two words. Renee Paris." She sat there silently for a very long time and didn't offer up anything else by way of explanation. She sniffled and blinked back some tears.

"Can you tell me about Jimmy's death?"

She got that distant look again and she spoke in almost a monotone, like she'd gone into a sort of trance just to protect herself. She was somewhere else, speaking in emotionless, almost rehearsed lines. It sounded like she was reading them without the slightest bit of comprehension.

"It was following the bankruptcy, after we'd lost our condo and the lake place. Both our cars had been repossessed and we were sharing a used Geo Metro we got for seven hundred bucks without brake lights or insurance. We were getting notices in the mail every day and threatening phone calls until ten at night. The calls were coming all day, seven days a week from collection agencies, credit card companies and then the tax people. All our credit cards had been cancelled. What little we had left was attached." She sort of came back to the present, sipped some tea and focused on me.

"I was working as a nurse's aide. By that time my income was garnished. I think I was bringing in about two-fifty a week. I was desperately trying to get into nursing school. Jimmy was attempting to start a consulting business," she scoffed. "Not that he had any clients willing to be consulted. We'd moved into a depressing, little efficiency apartment alongside the freeway near downtown. Then one day I guess it just got to be too much and he made the big leap." She sort of half smiled and stared at me in a strange way.

"They never found him, his body. I had to wait all this time before they paid on his life insurance. It was just last spring before he was declared legally dead. Seven years," she said and then she was somewhere else entirely. Certainly not in the same small, sparse living room with me.

"Mommy," a little voice suddenly called from the kitchen.

"I'm coming, honey," she answered, then quickly stood and left me sitting there alone.

I felt like I needed a drink after talking with Sue White, but not tea and just one wasn't going to do the

75

trick. I decided not to have any. I called Danielle and ended up leaving another message. Louie had already gone home or at least he wasn't in the office. I just sat in the dark for a long while, staring out the window and onto the frozen street at nothing.

Chapter Eighteen

I hadn't been in the office for much longer than a first cup of coffee when my phone rang. The second I heard that gum snapping on the other end of the line, before he even said his first word the bottom fell out of my day. Detective Norris Manning, homicide.

"Haskell."

"Detective Manning. How nice of you to call. Don't tell me, you're having a Christmas party and you'd like me to attend."

"Yeah, that's it, a celebration, sort of. You know you're always one step ahead of me, Haskell. How do you do it?" he said and snapped his gum a few more times.

I waited.

"I'd appreciate you swinging by, oh say in the neighborhood of three-fifteen this afternoon, just to chat."

"Chat. Should I have counsel present?"

"We're just chatting, Haskell, it's not like you're being charged or anything."

I waited, but he didn't add the word *'yet'*.

"Nothing we couldn't handle over the phone?" I probably sounded a little too hopeful.

"And miss seeing your smiling face down here, again?"

"Well, I mean, I know you're awfully busy."

"Never too busy to make time for you, Haskell."

"Well then, I wouldn't miss the opportunity, Detective. Your office? Or, should we meet at a neutral location? Maybe someplace we could both relax and feel at ease, enjoy one another's company?"

"No. Down here will suit me just fine. Three-fifteen," he growled and hung up.

I drummed my fingers on the desk for two more cups of coffee, racking my brain trying to figure out what it was. I hadn't done anything wrong on the insurance company applications. Holding Paris' head under the faucet? That didn't seem likely. Maybe the luke-warm pizza I brought over to Sue White last night.

I phoned Danielle and left another message. Then I phoned Louie and left a message for him, explaining Manning's phone call. I phoned my pal Lieutenant Aaron LaZelle, Manning's boss. Surprisingly, I got through.

"LaZelle."

"Aaron, Dev. How's it going?"

"You'll have to direct your questions to Detective Manning."

"Come on, man. I just wanted to wish you a Merry Christmas. Well, and maybe get a little heads up. I just wondered what Manning wanted to talk to me about?"

"Don't you think he would be the best one to answer that?"

"Manning? I was hoping you might shed some light. You know Manning and I go back a ways and well, it hasn't always been the most positive relationship. I was just thinking…"

"Don't."

78

"What?"

"Don't. Don't think, Dev. Just do. Be down here for your interview with the man, answer whatever he plans to ask you truthfully and then things seem to sort of have a way of working themselves out."

"Yeah, that's just what I'm worried about. Manning's on some case, any case and the first thing he thinks of is *'how can he pin whatever happened on me?'*"

"A little paranoid, are we?"

"You know the history."

"I know you've never been convicted of something you didn't do."

"That doesn't really make me feel any better."

"Which is something you should take up with Detective Manning. Sorry, I can't help. Anything else?"

"Well, yeah, now that you mention it, I..."

"Nice to talk with you, Dev," he said, then hung up. I didn't think it would help to call back and suggest we'd been disconnected.

Chapter Nineteen

I was stylishly late to my meeting with Detective Manning. The truth was, I didn't want to face Manning alone and I'd been trying to get hold of Louie, but I hadn't been able to reach him. I figured he was either still in court or drinking in some sleazy, tawdry dive and I wished I was with him. It was almost three-forty-five before I made it into the police station and announced myself to the Desk Sergeant.

"Oh yeah, Haskell, I thought that was you coming in. Yeah, Manning's called down a couple of times to see if you even bothered to show up. You know how he gets. Let me just buzz him and let him know you finally decided to pull the thumb out of your ass."

"Yeah, Detective Manning. Sergeant Gennaro. Yes, sir. Just now. I see. Well, I think that might be a little inappropriate, sir," he said then glanced over and chuckled.

"I could come back at another time," I said, nodding and trying to appear helpful.

Gennaro shook his head and sort of waved me off. "That would be best, Detective. You will? Okay, we'll wait down here. Yes, not a problem. Thank you, sir."

As Gennaro hung up the phone he shook his head again and mumbled, "Oh, boy." Then he looked at me, smiled sweetly and pointed to a line of orange plastic chairs pushed up against the far wall. The wall was covered with a large black and white mural of the St. Paul Police Force taken in about 1890. About thirty really rough looking guys and two horse drawn paddy wagons. "Just have a seat over there. Someone will be here to escort you up in a few minutes, Mr. Haskell."

Apparently, we had different perceptions of the term, *'a few minutes'*.

As I waited I was entertained by a cast of characters. There was a skinny woman with sky blue hair wearing hot pants, seamed stockings and sporting what looked like a fresh black eye wishing to report an assault.

Some drunken guy with his hands cuffed behind his back and a large officer on either arm entered the lobby, singing, "I've got friends in low places. I've got friends in low places, I've got..."

A neurotic, middle-aged woman in a full length fur coat and holding a small white dog wearing a matching fur coat wanted to report an accident that *'certainly wasn't her fault'*.

A police officer carrying a large box of what sounded like live chickens walked up to the counter, shook the box and shouted at Gennaro, "Dinner is served."

It was a few minutes after the second time I'd approached the counter and asked, "Do you think he forgot about me?" that a heavy set guy wearing a light colored sport coat and in need of a shave walked into the lobby.

"Mr. Haskell," he called out, like he was searching the crowd for me. I was the only one other than

81

Sergeant Gennaro sitting in the lobby. I sort of nodded and signaled with my index finger as I stood up.

He nodded back at me then walked over to a security door, punched in a code and waited for me to catch up. On the ride up in the elevator he didn't say anything. I think he was trying to rub the sleep from his eyes, running his large hands up and down over his red face and sighing a couple of times. I could hear a bristling sound as his hands ran over his unshaved face.

Just before the elevator doors opened he took a deep breath, and then assumed a stance like he was about to walk into a pit full of howling Rottweilers. I followed him out into the empty hallway and through another security door labeled *'Robbery/Homicide'*.

"Just grab a seat," he instructed. "I'll let Manning know you're waiting."

I saw no advantage to informing him Manning was aware I'd been waiting for the better part of the past hour, so I just sat down. I was going to joke with him about the lack of magazines in the little room, but figured now maybe wasn't the best time.

I'd been studying my feet and counting the floor tiles in the tiny room for what seemed like days when the door suddenly flew open and Manning called, "Haskell, get in here," like I'd been keeping him waiting.

He was in white shirtsleeves rolled half-way up his arm. A manila file was tucked under his left arm and he slurped from a coffee mug in his right hand. His head was red, redder than normal, whatever 'normal' was. Thankfully, not the crimson I'd seen it become a few times when he could grow apoplectic. He attacked the wad of gum in his mouth, causing it to snap every other second. The fringe of red hair running around the sides of his head looked to have been recently trimmed.

"I've got us right down here, in three," he said. He was quickly a half-dozen steps ahead of me and I guessed he was referring to interview room three.

I wasn't sure if 'three' meant that whatever my supposed offense was, it was more, or less serious than being in interview rooms one or two. I followed dutifully and he suddenly stepped into a room and held the door for me. The moment I was in the room he let go of the door and instructed me to, "have a seat there," indicating one of only two chairs, pointing with his coffee mug just as the door slammed shut.

He stood there watching me, snapping his gum impatiently while I pulled out the chair and sat down.

"What's this about, Detective?"

He seemed to ponder that for a bit before he ignored my question completely. He opened up his manila file and carefully positioned it in front of him. He took a moment and used both hands to line the edge of the file up squarely with the edge of the table.

The top sheet in the file had four images centered on the page. Each image was about two-and-a-half inches square. There was an eight digit number written in what looked like red marker on the upper right corner of the page and I took that to probably be a file or case number. There were multiple lines of copy printed below the images, but the print was too small to read, and well, it was upside down.

The images looked like building rubble from somewhere out of Syria. In one of the images the rear end of a car hung out from beneath a pile of bricks. Since I didn't know about any car bombings anywhere in the universe I began to relax for just a second or two before Manning looked up.

He stared at me for a long moment without saying anything, suggesting he was in charge, not me and he was just weighing his options on the best way to blind side me.

"So, Haskell. What have you been up to lately?"

"You dragged me down here to learn about my social life?"

"You're always up to something interesting, just a little curious, is all."

"Do I need counsel present? My lawyer?" I asked.

He sort of pursed his lips like he was taking my question seriously. Then his stare seemed to increase in intensity, he lowered his voice an octave and said very matter-of-fact, "I don't think so, we're just having a friendly little chat, is all. Just the two of us, you and me. You're not charged with anything, at least that I know of. I can check if you'd like?"

It wouldn't make a difference even if he did check. In fact, about all it would do would be to extend the time I'd have to sit in the room. Manning would probably forget about me and just leave me locked in here while he went home for the night.

"I've got nothing to hide."

He nodded, pretending he really believed me.

"Mind telling me where you've been the last few days?"

"Always in town. Let's see, I was at The Spot a couple of nights back, then home. I've got witnesses. I had an early dinner with a friend last night, witnesses. Three nights back I was at a friend's home until the following morning, maybe a little after the noon hour. Most days I've been in my office, you know, working."

"What are you currently working on?"

"Client confidentiality, I'm afraid. I really don't wish to discuss it any further than that, unless you have some sort of court order."

He looked at me as if to say, *'I can get a court order and a lot more, anytime I want.'*

Mercifully, there was a knock on the door and the same exhausted guy in the sport coat who brought me up in the elevator partially stepped into the room.

"Sorry to interrupt, I've got Mr. Haskell's attorney out here."

Louie suddenly squeezed past the guy and waddled in. He was wearing a wrinkled blue suit today, just a hint of bourbon floated along with him.

"I'm Mr. Laufen. Mr. Haskell's attorney. Detective Manning, I believe, correct?"

Manning nodded then flipped the file in front of him closed.

"We were just finishing up, here," he said.

"Don't stop on my account," Louie said.

"No, not a problem. Just some general questions on Haskell's whereabouts the past couple of days. I think we've got it sorted out, don't we, Haskell?"

I could have ranted about wasting my time, about doing this over the phone, about keeping me waiting downstairs in the lobby. Instead, I just nodded and said, "Yes." And left it at that.

"Can't thank you enough for your time," Manning said, then walked over and held the door for us as we exited the room.

Chapter Twenty

"I'll have another," **Louie** said as he pushed his empty glass across the bar then turned back toward me. "You sure you don't have any idea?"

"No, I don't. Honest. Like I told you, I waited down in that stupid lobby for close to an hour, maybe longer. Manning had me in that interview room for all of two or three minutes before you came in. I'm telling you, that guy just has a hard-on for me. Any heinous crime that comes down the road his first thought is how in the hell he can tie it to me."

"And those pictures you saw in his file?"

"Bombed out building from what I could tell. Looked like something out of Syria or Iraq. You know I'm not involved with anything or anyone even remotely associated with that sort of political shit. I've been checking employment dates on insurance company job applications for God's sake."

"What about Renee Paris?"

"That gig was just sort of for a friend. In fact, I told her she'd be better served getting a lawyer and going to court. Not that she has any sort of case to begin with. Last I checked, Paris was still ignoring any request to contact her and, well, that's where it stands."

Louie shook his head and sipped. "Something's up. I know you're not a fan of Manning, but he doesn't waste time, he's good."

"Well, he sure as hell wasted my time today, that's for damn sure."

"And you said you talked to Paris?"

"Well, yeah."

Louie must have picked up on my tone and he shot me a look. "What the hell does that mean? What'd you do, Dev?"

"Nothing, really. He was just being a prick is all and we may have exchanged some words."

"Anything else?" He looked at me like my dad used to do when he already knew about whatever stupid stunt I'd pulled.

"I may have sort of pushed him or something."

"Define something?"

"Okay, he yelled at me, called me names. I sort of grabbed him and maybe splashed some water on him."

"What?"

"It just sort of happened, the water was running in the kitchen sink, he was being a jerk and well…"

"Water?"

"Yeah."

"Christ, is he okay? Did you try to drown him? Water board? What? I mean, was he breathing?"

"Oh yeah, nothing like that. He might have been, you know, burned, sort of, a little bit pink, maybe. But he was alive and mostly okay when I left."

"Exactly how hot was it? Scalding?"

"I guess it could have been."

"Are you kidding me, scalding? Where did you do this, his house? His office? A men's room?"

"Casey's."

"Casey's?"

"That joint that closed a couple of years back, you remember? Turns out jerk-off Paris owns the place, or at least the building. He was in there cooking up his Bar-B-Que sauces. See, apparently he's started this business called LuSifer's…"

"Wait a minute, Casey's, you mean the place that just burned down the other night?"

"Huh?"

"Oh, Christ Dev. Casey's burned down a couple of days ago. The whole thing, the fire, it's under investigation."

I suddenly remembered the images in Manning's file. One of them had the tale end of a car sticking out from beneath a pile of rubble. Had I seen a Mercedes logo on the trunk of that car? I wasn't sure, maybe I was making that up. After all, I'd been looking at the damn images upside down.

"Perfect timing once again, Dev. You're there, assaulting the sleaziest con-man in town and the next thing you know the place gets burned to the ground."

"How would Manning even know I'd been there?"

"Gee, let me think, maybe for starters Renee Paris told him."

Chapter Twenty-One

Danielle still hadn't answered any of my phone calls. I placed two more last night while Louie and I sat at the bar and tried to figure out what in the hell was going on. We never did come up with anything. I sent her a text message before I went to bed and another one when I woke up this morning. I got nothing back in return for my trouble.

I was beginning to wonder if maybe Renee Paris had somehow gotten hold of her. Maybe he was desperate enough or just plain mad enough to break into that museum she lived in. Or, maybe he followed her to one of her *'beautiful people'* soirees and chose a convenient place to grab her. I decided to drive over to her house to see if she was okay, check the place out and well, offer any other service she might be in need of.

Danielle's red-brick Victorian barn sat on the corner lot of a street filled with similar Victorian barns. When the place had been built, over a century ago, it had been situated on a bluff that overlooked the rooftops of a tranquil working class neighborhood made up of German and Czech families. They worked in the breweries, green houses and bakeries. They built churches, raised families and in general added to the quality of life in our growing river town. Their tree lined streets beneath the bluff flowed lazily off in the distance toward the Mississippi river.

Forty years ago the state, in its wisdom, slashed through the tranquil neighborhood with a four lane freeway and thirty foot high concrete sound barriers. The din from the traffic of folks racing past twenty-four/seven provided a constant undercurrent of mechanical screech. Thirty years ago Dutch elm disease wiped out all the trees along the streets and denuded the entire neighborhood. The view of the river valley was cut in half ten years ago by a new hundred-foot concrete tower belching smoke from the power plant. Such is progress.

The heater was working in the Lincoln as I pulled in front of Danielle's home. I phoned her from the comfort of my front seat.

"Hi, thanks for calling, but I'm unable to take your call right now. Please leave a message and I'll get back to you just as soon as possible. Bye, bye."

"Danielle, Dev Haskell. Give me a call. I want to make sure you're all right," I said then hung up. God, I didn't want to step outside my car. It was about eight degrees below zero and windy. The wind chill was something like minus twenty, but out I went anyway, just to be a good guy.

I damn near died of exposure on her front porch after ringing the doorbell a half dozen times and waiting for someone to answer the door. Then I walked around the entire house. The place looked secure, no open or broken windows, the back door and a side door were securely locked. There weren't any footprints in the snow suggesting someone had been casing the place or had tried to break in. I attempted to look in the garage, but the windows had been blacked out and both the overhead and the side garage doors were locked.

I went back onto her front porch and rang the door bell again. Her mail dropped into a slot next to the front door. I peered into the front entry through the beveled glass panels on either side of the door, but I couldn't spot anything that looked like a pile of mail. I don't know, maybe she was at a yoga class or she had scurried back to Tuscany with girlfriends. I was just about frozen stiff so I hurried back into my car and fired it up. Thankfully, the heat came on a minute or two later.

I decided I would drive past Casey's and look at the rubble. I was thinking about the news cast I caught for all of a few seconds the other night. The images of the firemen with the icicles hanging from their helmets must have been the fire at Casey's.

I circled the block where the building used to stand. I drove around twice. There wasn't much to see. We'd had an inch or two of snow each of the past few nights, not much, but enough to cover everything. Now the site was just a series of gently rolling little piles of rubble. The occasional beam stuck out a few feet into the air, but there was nothing that would really grab your attention.

One thing caught my eye. There wasn't the rear end of a car to be found, anywhere. I guessed the police probably pulled the thing out and brought it to the crime lab to run more tests.

When I got back to the office I went online and watched the archive footage of the news reports, then went through the articles in both the St. Paul and Minneapolis papers. I didn't read anything I didn't already know. The building was a total loss. There was

91

no mention of Renee Paris anywhere in the articles or the newscast.

Chapter Twenty-Two

I searched online to try and get a handle on where Renee Paris may have landed. The only thing I could find was outdated information directing me to the vacant, soon-to-be foreclosed structure over by the Witches Hat tower.

A sleaze ball like Paris, there had to be a million places he could hide. The only thing I was pretty sure of was, wherever he ended up, it would be high class. I fooled around online for another few hours and came up with absolutely nothing. I didn't want to be a pest, or a bigger pest than I'd already been, so I didn't phone Danielle. If she hadn't responded to the half dozen phone messages or any of my text messages I figured one more wasn't going to do the trick. I phoned Heidi instead.

"Hi, Dev, and no, I'm busy tonight."

"What?"

"You heard me, I'm busy. I'm out with the girls."

"The girls? Or some new, self-absorbed flake who'll drive you nuts before the night is over. Who was the last guy? That Waldo character."

"Oh, jealous? His name was Destin, by the way, and yeah, he did kind of look like Waldo, didn't he?"

93

"He always wore that red and white stripped shirt that even said, *'Where's Waldo?'*. I don't know, you tell me."

"Well, it doesn't matter. The answer is still no. Really I'm going out with the girls. We're all meeting at Bunnies."

"You're kidding?"

"Why? Don't tell me *you've* been there? It's kind of classy. I didn't think it was the sort of place you would…"

"No, I haven't been there. As a matter of fact someone called me from the ladies room there."

"No thanks, I don't need to hear another one of your perverted stories, Dev, so just stop right there."

"That's it, she just called me. Said my name was written on the door of the stall in the Ladies room. One of those *'For a good time call'* sort of deals."

"Oh, you're kidding, that is sort of funny. Why did you do that? Write your name in the Ladies room."

"I didn't write my name in the Ladies room, some other idiot did."

"Hmm-mmm, we'll have to check it out. Anyway, some other time, darling."

I'd fallen asleep on my couch watching a rerun of a Netflix movie I hated the first time I watched it when my phone rang.

"Hello, Haskell In…"

"Oh, good, you're still up." It was Heidi. Guessing from the 'Woo-hoo-hoo' noise in the background she was still out with her girlfriends.

"Umm, yeah, just going over some files here."

"Sure you were. Hey, are you okay to give me a lift? I just think I probably shouldn't drive. I mean, as long as you haven't been drinking. If that's okay?"

Not really, but it beat sleeping on the couch in front of this stupid movie. And of course the added potential of a Heidi benefit. "Yeah, where are you? You still down at Bunnies?"

"Yep," she said then I heard what sounded like her taking a very large sip of something I figured wouldn't be lemonade.

"You just stay there, I'm on the way. I'll come in and get you."

"Thanks, bye, bye, bye," she said and returned to the festivities.

I walked into Bunnies about a half-hour later. The place was just about empty, after all, most normal people were either working tomorrow or looking for work and they'd all gone home by now.

"Sorry, sir, we've already had last call," the bartender said. He carried two stacks of pint beer glasses, one in each hand. Each stack looked to be about thirty glasses high and rose above his shoulders. He kept moving toward a corner of the bar and added the glasses to the dozens already arranged on the counter.

"Not a problem, just here to pick someone up," I said, then pointed at the group of five women seated at the only occupied table in the place.

"Oh, thanks, man." He sounded like he really meant it and continued stacking glasses.

Their table was littered with a number of different colored paper bags with bits of fancy tissue hanging out of them. The bags probably contained little gifts they could all complain about when they got home. I noticed what looked like a number of empty Prosecco bottles scattered amongst the bags and thought, *'Oh-oh.'*

"Hi, Heidi," I said. I had to repeat myself over the high pitched laughing. "Heidi, your limo awaits."

Heidi turned, looked up at me bleary eyed and slowly focused. "Hi, Dev, perfect timing it's your turn to buy."

Everyone giggled and reached for their glasses.

"Yeah, not that I didn't already try, but unfortunately they've had last call and I can't. I really wish I could, honest. Nothing I'd like to do more than buy a round."

"You sure?"

"Very."

"Well, come on girls, our ride is here. We'll just go somewhere else." She giggled then drained close to half a glass. They all followed suit and slowly got to their feet, pulling on coats and hats. Apparently, I was going to be everyone's designated driver.

"Where are you parked?" Heidi asked.

"Outside," I said, which seemed to satisfy her.

"Thank you, thanks, bye, bye," they all chorused to the bartender as they filed past on the way out the door.

"Thanks ladies," he said. Then looked at me, nodded and seemed to wish a silent *'good luck'*.

Paper bags and tissue rustled as they made their way into the winter night. Once outside the fifteen below temp slapped us in the face. Everyone scurried across the parking lot toward my car, giggling.

One of the girls said, "Oh my God you guys, look at his car, you're kidding. What's with these doors? And what's gone on in this back seat?"

"They're called suicide doors. They're coming back in style. Hop in, ladies, before we all die of exposure."

This was followed by loud, collective laughter.

It was forty minutes later when we dropped the last one off, Karen. She said the same thing all the others had as they exited. "Bye, thanks for the ride, Dev. Call me tomorrow, Heidi, we'll talk." Meaning, I guessed, a lot more than simple, casual conversation. I drove off once she made it in her front door.

"Oh, thanks, Dev. That was nice of you. Did you have fun?"

"That's what I was going to ask you. Did you have a good time?"

"I had a great time."

"I'm thinking it's late and we're actually closer to my place. Want to sleep over?" I tried not to sound too overly hopeful.

She got this snide little smile on her face and said, "Sleep? Really? I think we might be able to think of something better to do than sleep."

'Yes!' I thought.

Chapter Twenty-Three

Ten minutes later we were pulling into my driveway. I gently shook Heidi awake. "Heidi, come on. There's a nice warm bed upstairs we can both climb into. Wake up, honey."

"Oh, God, bed sounds wonderful," she said, but she said it in a way that made me think we were suddenly on opposite wave lengths.

She was sound asleep when I came out of the bathroom. I heard that deep Prosecco induced breathing, remembered the elbow she gave me the last time I'd attempted to wake her and knew there was no point in trying. I'd have to wait until morning.

"Dev, Dev, wake up. Come on, wake up."

It was music to my ears as she gently shook me awake, no doubt unable to control her passion and wait any longer. My patience was finally paying off and this was going to be worth it. I rolled over and focused on Heidi sitting on the edge of my bed. She appeared to have showered and was completely dressed. In fact, she'd already pulled on her winter coat.

"What time is it? What the…"

"Come on, get dressed, you have to drive me back to Bunnies so I can get my car. I've got a client coming

98

in at nine this morning and I have to go home and change."

"Could we just take a few minutes here and…"

"No, come on, I mean it. Besides, I've already showered. I gotta get going," she said and stood up.

I lay in bed for half a second, thinking *'This can't be happening. I don't believe it.'*

"Dev, come on, I told you I'm not kidding, get going," she said. She checked herself briefly in the mirror before she walked out of my bedroom. She called again as she headed downstairs. "Dev."

Heidi was the first one to finally speak as we drove to her car. "Oh, God, you big baby, will you please quit pouting. I'll make it up to you," she said. We were just a minute or two away from the parking lot at Bunnies. Heidi was brushing on makeup using the mirror hanging from the back of my passenger seat visor.

"Sure, not a problem. I mean, I interrupted my night. I stopped working. I drove down to Bunnies. I gave all your girlfriends a ride home. My ears are still hurting from the noise level in the car." I shot her a glance.

"Maybe if the heat had come on we wouldn't have had to talk so loud. God, everyone was frozen half to death. We had to talk just to stay warm."

"Hey, you called me. Like I said, I was working."

"Sure you were," she said and just let that hang there for a couple of blocks. "Hey, you know what? Did I tell you about the ladies room? Remember you told me you got that client because your name was written on the door of the bathroom stall?"

"Yeah, Danielle. She's the one who called me from Bunnies."

"Well, it isn't there now. We checked."

99

"Not there? My name and phone number? They probably wiped it off when they were cleaning."

"Could be, but if they wiped it off they didn't bother to remove any of the other stuff written in there."

"Maybe you were in the wrong stall."

"There's only three. We all traipsed in there to check it out. I told the girls about it and they thought it was so funny they just had to see it. We looked all over and never found it."

"So you didn't see my phone number and then it said, *'call for a good time'*?"

"Nope."

"She said it was just below the hook on the door, where you hang your coat."

"Nope, honest, we really checked. Karen wanted to take a picture of it and post it on Facebook. Oh, hey, there's my car, see? Over by the side of the building."

There were two other abandoned cars in the lot. I knew Heidi's. It was a white Lexus. It was the only white Lexus in the lot and I pulled alongside of the thing.

"Have a great meeting," I said, not meaning a word.

"Oh, get over it. I said I'll make it up to you."

"If it wasn't really good I wouldn't care, okay, Heidi. Just saying."

She looked at me for a long moment. "You're sort of sweet, in your own warped little way. Is that all you ever think about?" She leaned over and gave me a quick kiss, ran her hand suggestively up and down my inner thigh right before she grabbed me, then quickly jumped out of my car.

"That's not fair," I shouted.

She leaned back in, blew me a kiss and said, "Get the heater fixed in this bomb." Then she gave a quick wave, jumped inside her Lexus and locked the door.

Chapter Twenty-Four

I didn't feel like going back home and cooking breakfast, so I pulled into Moe's. On the way in I bought a copy of the Pioneer Press from the box out on the sidewalk.

"Just coming home from last night?" Bruce asked. He was Moe's manager and he was standing at the cash register, greeting all the working stiffs who didn't have to be in their office until nine.

"I wish. No, I enjoy the below freezing temperature so much, I decided not to miss another minute and came down to see you."

He smiled and shook his head like I'd just confirmed a number of his misgivings. I sipped some coffee before I unfolded the newspaper. The front headline glared back at me. **Human Remains Discovered**. There was a photo, similar to the ones Manning had the other day in his file. It looked just like what I'd seen when I'd driven back over to Casey's, some snow covered rubble with a couple of beams sticking out.

The article didn't say much, other than evidence of human remains had been found. Well, that and the fact that the intensity of the blaze was leading firefighters to

102

believe some form of accelerant had been used. In layman's terms that meant someone had set the fire. And then either they got caught up in the thing and burned, or quite possibly some idiot had set the fire in an attempt to dispose of a body.

Either option and maybe a half dozen others were possible, especially when you threw that sleaze ball Renee Paris into the equation. None of which seemed to work in my favor. I figured it was a pretty safe guess this was what had been behind Manning's phone call and brief interview the other day. The question was how had he come up with my name? I had to be one of at least a thousand people who wanted a piece of Renee Paris and most of them would have a better reason than me to put the guy down.

Before I had my jacket hung up in the office, Louie started giving me the third degree. He was attired in a slightly less-wrinkled pinstripe suit. The suit coat was hung crookedly over the back of his chair in such a way that the left-hand sleeve dragged along the floor. The wheel of his desk chair had come to sit squarely on top of the sleeve. The knot on his tie hung loosely a couple of inches below his chins.

"You hear the latest, Dev?"

"We're out of coffee?" I replied, staring at the empty pot.

"No, I was just hoping you'd show up to make some. But, did you hear the news? About that fire?"

"I read it in the paper this morning."

"You're kidding?" he said, sounding more than a little surprised.

"I read the paper, I keep up on things."

"Yeah, sure. Anyway, I'd say that was behind your pal Manning's little inquiry yesterday."

"Probably, although he never mentioned it specifically. Still, those images I saw in his file…"

"Yeah, that was planned. He wanted to see if they'd get you talking, maybe make you say something incriminating."

"Like what? *'I did it.'* Not likely. Besides I didn't do anything. If it was Paris they found in that rubble half this city probably has a better motive than anything I could come up with."

"I'm thinking it was Paris who got fried in that place. You didn't smell anything like propane, see a stack of newspapers or something by the stove, maybe a gas can?"

"No, I told you, he was cooking Bar-B-Que sauce. Had five or six of these big containers on the stove when I got there. The things were on the boil, place smelled great, actually."

"I think it would be a good idea, I'm speaking as your lawyer here, to call Manning. Make a statement as to what you saw. Let him know you were there and that there was an incident."

"An incident. Christ, he'd love to run with that. I'm already guilty of every crime in the book with that guy. I don't know, as far as he's concerned it's just a matter of time before he nails me."

"This whole thing ain't sounding right, Dev, and he knows you were there. Did you ever hear back from that woman?"

"Danielle?"

Louie nodded.

"No. I've left about a hundred phone messages. I sent her text messages. Even went over there and checked the place out. She wasn't there. Hell, she could have left town or just gone to the grocery store. I don't know."

"You'd think she would at least return a phone call."

"Maybe. She's sort of one of those ditzy types."

"Ditzy types?"

"I think she's got a trust fund. You know, she wakes up in her inherited mansion on the first of every month and there's money in the bank. Then she tells you how busy she's been shopping or traveling and she's clueless to what working stiffs have to do day in and day out."

Louie nodded like he knew the type. "It would still be a good idea to phone Manning. Get your side of the story on the record. I'll go down there with you."

"My side of the story? There isn't even a story."

"Pretty safe bet the cops think there is. Probably no way they've gotten an I.D. this fast on whoever got roasted in there. Hell, that could be weeks or even months, depending on what they're dealing with."

"Like I said, I'm thinking its most likely Paris."

"Maybe, maybe not. The fact is you, me, the cops, no one knows at this stage. Let's just get out in front of the problem and get this nailed down before you have someone working off all sorts of speculations that seem to land on your doorstep. Speculations that we can eliminate right here and now once you get a statement on the record."

"Does it have to be Manning?"

"You said it yourself that he's the one out to get you. Wouldn't it seem to make the most sense to point him in a different direction?"

"I guess, Jesus. Okay, okay, let me make some coffee and then I'll call him."

"I tell you what, you call him and I'll make the coffee."

Chapter Twenty-Five

Up to this point my dealings with Detective Norris Manning had pretty much been less than positive. Once he learned it was me on the phone his usual routine was to keep me on hold for ten or fifteen minutes just for fun before he hung up.

"Who shall I say is calling?" the woman asked in a slight accent. I guess she was the switchboard operator. The call was probably routed through India or some distant place so the city could save money and not employ a local.

"Devlin Haskell. I spoke to Detective Manning the other day. I'm calling to try and set up an appointment with him." I looked over at Louie. His back was to me. Part of a wrinkled shirt tail hung out over his belt and he was nodding as he dumped a half dozen measured spoons of coffee grounds into the machine sitting on top of the file cabinet.

"I'll see if Detective Manning is available. One moment please."

I waited for ten seconds and was about to hang up when the sound of snapping gum crackled across the line and a voice half-yelled, "Manning."

"Detective Manning, this is Dev Haskell."

106

Louie pushed the 'ON' button on the coffee pot then turned to face me, nodding his support.

"Haskell, how nice," Manning said, sounding like he didn't mean one word.

"Listen, Detective. I read the morning paper."

"Oh?"

"Yeah, the front page article about the fire that happened at the Casey's site."

"Oh?"

"Yes, sir, I'd like to make an appointment with you so I can come in with my attorney, Mr. Laufen, and…"

"I remember your attorney, Mr. Laufen."

"Yeah, I figured you might. Anyway, I'd like to come down and set the record straight."

Louie shook his head and placed a finger to his lips, signaling me to be quiet.

"Which record are we talking about, Haskell? I really have trouble keeping up where you're concerned."

"We'd like to make an appointment to come down there, Detective. The sooner, the better," I added.

Louie nodded approval.

"I can fit you in at, oh, how does twelve-forty-five sound?"

It didn't sound surprising, considering the source. It would screw up our lunch time plans, not that I had any.

"That works," I said, trying to sound like it did. "We'll see you then, twelve-forty-five."

"Thank you," Manning said, sounding less than sincere before he hung up.

"So?" Louie asked.

"You heard, twelve-forty-five. Typical, just in time to screw up our lunch time, plus it gives him a couple

107

of hours to plan on how he can best rake me over the coals."

"Come on, how long does it take to order a Big Mac and fries? We can go through the drive-up if we want. Besides, he's going to take your statement. Not give you the third degree."

"You sound a lot more convinced of that than me," I said.

It was a couple hours later and we were grabbing an early lunch. "Can you give me an extra ketchup with those fries?" Louie said. "You want anything else?" he asked me.

I shook my head *'no'*.

"Better throw in a McRib," Louie said.

"Will there be anything else, sir?"

"Probably one of those apple pies too," Louie added, and looked over at me. "You sure you don't want anything else?"

I shook my head again.

"That'll do it," he said into the speaker.

The guy gave us our total and told us to pull up to the first window. We pulled up and waited for the car ahead to finish. The woman appeared to be having trouble finding her exact change.

"I figure the apple pie kind of takes care of the fruit requirement for the day," Louie said, sounding serious. He was staring vacantly out the window at the car ahead of us. Now the woman was placing one coin at a time into the palm of the guy's outstretched hand.

"Yeah, after the Big Mac, large fries, cheeseburger and the McRib is washed down with that strawberry shake, something healthy like apple pie probably does make sense," I said.

Louie nodded then added, "I'm getting this, by the way, you paid the last time." The car ahead finally

108

moved and Louie drove forward until he was alongside the window.

The guy inside was talking into a headset, taking an order as he sorted a handful of coins into the change drawer. He took the twenty dollar bill Louie gave him, handed back about six cents in change and told us to pull ahead to the next window.

As nice as Louie's gesture sounded I felt like reminding him that the last time we ate together I paid after we had spent the better part of four hours at some trendy Italian place with thirty dollar entrees, two bottles of wine, something flaming for dessert and pretty strong after dinner drinks. I was not going to consider us even.

"Thanks," Louie said a moment later and handed a very large bag over to me. He pulled an empty coffee cup out of the console between us, tossed it over his shoulder and into the back seat. Then he crammed his strawberry shake into the console, loosening the plastic lid in the process.

I stared into the bag. It figured. My filet of fish was way down on the bottom beneath everything Louie had ordered. "What do you want first?" I asked.

"I don't care, just hand me something," he said, then drove off. He started with the apple pie, wolfed down the cheeseburger, and then inhaled the Big Mac after that. He let the wrappers drift down to the floor around his feet. He was working his way through the McRib, dribbling sauce on his pinstriped lapel when he asked, "Mmm-mmm, what's wrong, aren't you gonna eat?"

He said it in a way that suggested he wasn't really worried about my food intake, but was maybe thinking there could be one more thing to devour if somehow I had lost my appetite.

109

"Yes, I'm going to eat. It's just that my filet of fish was way down on the bottom. Your stuff was piled on top. I couldn't get to the thing until now."

"Don't know how you can eat that thing," he said and gave a non-committal shrug. As we pulled into the potholed parking lot across from the police station Louie reached for his strawberry shake.

"God, I thought they were supposed to pave this damn thing," he said just as the lid slipped off and strawberry shake dripped over the McRib sauce he'd spilled on his suit coat.

"You're dripping there, big boy."

"Huh? Oh, damn it," he said, then bounced across two more potholes and pulled into a parking place. He crammed the cup back into the console then used his index finger to halt strawberry shake from running any further down his suit coat. He licked his finger clean, repositioned the lid on the shake and started sucking the straw in earnest.

I placed my Filet of Fish back in the box. I'd lost my appetite and truth be told I wasn't looking forward to heading back into the police station and talking with Manning.

Louie released his grip on the straw long enough to ask, "You gonna finish that fish?"

"You can have it if you want."

"God, I don't know why anyone orders these things," he said and crammed half the filet into his mouth. "Mmm-mmm," he grunted, then sort of nodded and raised his eyebrows as if to suggest, *'not half-bad'*.

"Should we go in there and get this over with?" I said a few minutes later.

Louie sucked on his straw until it gurgled an empty reply. He dropped the cup into the back seat and looked over at me. "Just pay attention to my cues in there.

Okay? We are here of our own free will. We're here to help in their investigation. We're here to take you off their list of suspects. Anytime Manning asks you a question I want you to look at me before you answer. I touch you on the leg like this," he touched my thigh. "That means you shut the hell up. I don't care if you're in mid-sentence, Dev. You stop talking. Got it?"

I nodded.

"Say it," Louie commanded.

"Yeah, relax, I got it. Come on, Manning's probably running a stop watch just to see if we show up on time." I climbed out of the car. Louie did the same, scattering wrappers across the floor of the front seat as he did so. He sort of hiked his trousers up by pulling on his belt, not that it did anything to help his appearance. He strode off toward the building entrance across the street. I followed dutifully behind. I focused on the graveled parking lot, dodging potholes until we made it to the street. Louie stamped his feet on the pavement in an effort to knock off some of the snow and slush.

"Just remember, we're in charge on this deal. We're here to set the record straight and get ahead of any bullshit ideas before they get carried away over the course of their investigation," Louie said, then stepped off again once a car drove past.

I noticed for the first time that his pinstriped coat had substantially thinner stripes than the stripes on his trousers. Somehow, he'd managed to mix up two different pinstriped suits. I figured that was the least of my problems as we entered the lobby and approached the Desk Sergeant.

Chapter Twenty-Six

We weren't incarcerated in the standard cinder block interview room with uncomfortable plastic chairs, whips, chains and torture devices hanging from the wall. Manning had us seated in a sort of conference room with padded carpet, a long polished wooden table, comfortable upholstered chairs and halfway decent coffee.

Aaron LaZelle had poked his head in as we were getting seated. We'd exchanged one liners, he thanked us for coming down and then he fled the scene as fast as was prudently possible.

Up until now, Manning hadn't said a lot except to explain that we were being taped and filmed. He introduced the dour faced blonde woman seated next to him as, "One of our department consultants, Ms. Sinn."

"That's S-I-N-N," she interjected with a slight growl and without the trace of a smile.

"Pleased to meet you," Louie said. He extended his wrinkled coat arm with a drop or two of strawberry shake.

"Nice to meet you." I nodded from across the table.

"So, let's get started, shall we?" Manning said. He looked about as comfortable with Ms. Sinn as I felt. He listed off the usual time and place information, the names of everyone in the room. He stated that we had come of our own free will and that I was not facing any charges, and on and on. Then he asked, "Does everything I've said so far meet with your approval?"

I nodded.

Louie said, "Yes, it does."

"I'm sorry, Mr. Haskell you gave a nod, would you mind stating for the record that you're in agreement thus far?"

"Yes, I agree to the time, the date and the names of everyone in this room." I half laughed.

Louie's hand gave me a warning shot beneath the table.

"Very well. If you would care to proceed with your statement, please."

I looked over at Louie and he nodded, giving me the go ahead.

"I was hired by a client to locate Mr. Renee Paris. Up until I spoke with my client I was only vaguely aware of Mr. Paris from local news reports. I had never met the man. To the best of my knowledge, I have never been involved in any business or social dealings with Renee Paris. I have never, to the best of my knowledge, been involved in a transaction of any sort with Renee Paris nor any organization he has been or is associated with."

I went on to describe how I searched the internet for information. How I reviewed his county tax records online. I stated that the real estate tax information is a matter of public record. Then I explained how I phoned him and set up an appointment to meet him. I stressed that Renee Paris suggested we meet at the Casey's location. I met with him, left and did not learn about the fire until forty-eight hours after the event when I read

113

about it in the newspaper. Once I read the newspaper article I phoned Detective Manning so I could make a statement. I finished and glanced over at Louie who gave me a brief nod.

"What did you hope to accomplish by meeting Mr. Paris?" Manning asked.

"Exactly what I did accomplish. I merely reminded him that my client had provided him with a loan and that my client wished to be paid back. I suggested to Mr. Paris that he might contact my client and work out some sort of payment arrangement."

"And your client is?"

Louie tapped me on the thigh and said, "I think we'll assert out right to client confidentiality at this point. Perhaps, if we can receive prior approval, we would be more than willing to pass that name on to you, Detective."

The humorless Sinn woman scribbled a note and slid it over to Manning, then stared at Louie's stained suit coat without blinking. I was beginning to think she might be more dangerous than Manning.

"Could you describe your conversation with Mr. Paris in a little more detail?" Manning asked.

"There really isn't that much to describe. He was cooking his Bar-B-Que sauce, at least that's what I think he was doing. LuSifer's is or well, maybe was his brand name."

Louie touched my leg again. "I'd like to point out that at this stage that's really just conjecture on the part of Mr. Haskell. He's unaware of circumstances that would lead one to conclude Mr. Paris is anything other than fit and continuing with his Bar-B-Que sauce business. Let the record state that LuSifer's *is* the brand name of Mr. Paris' sauce."

Manning nodded. "So noted. You were saying?"

Louie gave me a go ahead nod.

"Well, I was saying Paris was cooking up all this sauce. The place smelled great, there was a table covered with onion skins, boxes that looked like they had tomatoes in them, jars of spice, garlic, wrappers from pounds of butter, brown sugar. You know, the normal sort of stuff you'd have around if you were cooking, just lots of it."

Manning nodded like we were just pals shooting the shit.

"I think there were five or six large containers, maybe this big." I indicated with my hands. "They were cooking on the stove. I remember you could just hear this soft sort of boiling sound and like I said, the place smelled pretty good."

"Were you aware of any other individuals present?"

"No, to the best of my knowledge, it was just the two of us. I parked next to his car. At least I think it was his, a silver Mercedes. There were no other cars in the back lot. Only one set of footprints in the snow going up to the door. Like I said, I think we were alone, at least to the best of my knowledge."

The Sinn woman slid another note over to Manning.

Manning's face flushed slightly and looked like he was about to get mad. I couldn't determine if it was me or the note passing Sinn he was going to be mad at.

"Let's go back to your discussion with Mr. Paris, shall we? You suggested to Mr. Paris that your client wished to be repaid?"

"Yes."

"Did this seem to come as a surprise to Mr. Paris?"

"No, as a matter of fact I don't think he was surprised at all. I just..." Louie's hand hit off my thigh.

Manning looked from me to Louie, then back to me again.

"So, he just nodded and said thank you?" Manning finally asked.

"Not exactly, but I don't believe he was surprised. He mentioned something about insurance benefits and I suggested my client might want to be repaid in a more timely manner. Beyond that, whatever arrangement he works out with my client is strictly between the two of them. I don't believe my involvement would serve any purpose."

"Sounds like you've pretty much fulfilled whatever obligation you had to your client, fair comment?"

I nodded. "Yes, I delivered the message to Mr. Paris."

"And then you just walked out?"

Shit. "Pretty much, we may have said something else, exchanged pleasantries. I really can't recall, but nothing of substance."

"Pleasantries?"

Louie's hand hit my leg.

"Like I said, Detective, I told Mr. Paris my client wished to be repaid. I told him my client would consider payment arrangements and I pretty much left it at that."

Manning nodded. "Do you find it strange that the restaurant there, Casey's had been closed for some time and apparently the utilities were still on?"

"I wouldn't know anything about that."

"But the lights were on and Paris was cooking on the stove, you stated as much. Correct?"

I nodded, not liking what I feared lurked just around the corner.

"Do you recall, was that a gas stove?"

"I wouldn't know."

116

"Well, you said he had a number of pots on the boil, large containers, you said. About this big, five or six of them." He indicated the size of the containers with his hands just like I had done earlier.

"Yes."

"So, if they were on the boil, as you said, there must have been a gas flame or an electric burner. Correct?"

I began to relax. "Yes, I think it was a gas burner, now that you mention it. It was one of those large industrial stoves. I mean, the place was a restaurant." I half chuckled and looked at Manning and Sinn for a reaction. I didn't get one.

Manning nodded like he was processing new information, then he suddenly bore into me with icy blue eyes. "What about the kitchen sink?"

Shit. Shit. Shit.

Louie hit my leg, hard and said, "I think we've been fairly clear regarding what my client does or does not know, Detective. You have our statement. I think at this point its fairly obvious Mr. Haskell is willing to help in this investigation in any way he can. However, even Mr. Haskell has his limits. I would guess a simple call to Xcel energy would answer any questions you might have regarding the utility situation."

Manning focused on Louie for a moment. Sinn scribbled a note and slid it over to Manning. When he looked at the note his face grew just a little more red.

"Thank you for making time, Detective. Should you need any further cooperation on the part of Mr. Haskell I would appreciate it if you would contact me. With Mr. Haskell's busy work schedule I think I'll be able to serve as a more effective 'first point of contact'." As he rose to his feet Louie pulled a business card out of his mismatched suit coat and handed it to Manning.

"Thank you for your time, nice to meet you Ms. Sinn, this concludes our statement. Thank you. Dev?" Louie gave me a *'get your ass in gear'* look and we hurried out the door.

"Jesus Christ," I said in the elevator.

Louie signaled with his hand and I stopped talking. We waited until we were in his car and a block away before either one of us spoke.

"Where are you taking me for dinner?" Louie asked as he floored it and ran a yellow light.

"You can't possibly be hungry?"

"Not really, but I need something."

"How about The Spot?"

"Perfect," he said.

Chapter Twenty-Seven

Mike was bartending and Louie signaled him for another round before he turned back toward me. "The thing I don't get is that woman."

"Sinn?"

"Yeah, if she was acting as counsel for the department, and that's unusual, she was sure going about it in a funny way."

"How so? She just seemed like another pain in the ass lawyer. No offense."

Louie shook his head, suggesting he took no offense. "That note passing nonsense, what the hell? Lawyers, we all like to hear ourselves talk. Even if it's in a whisper. A little word or two scribbled on a note? That seems pretty strange to me. I'm going to check her out."

"Maybe she just needs to have her ashes hauled."

"That's your answer to everything, isn't it, Dev?"

I shrugged and nodded, it seemed so simple. "Hey, I gotta hit the can, I'll be back in a minute," I said and slid off the stool.

There was a drunk guy in the men's room. Let me rephrase that, there was a fat, really drunk guy in the men's room. He was standing in front of the urinal, the

119

only urinal, weaving back and forth. Although there'd been a smoking ban in Minnesota since forever, this clown had a cigarette going with about a half inch ash hanging off the end of the thing. I'd been here before, dealing with drunks, and I decided to just keep quiet.

He was weaving back and forth, which did nothing to help his aim. He placed a hand against the wall in front of him to steady himself. Then he looked down, at which point the ash fell and, judging from the way he jumped and screamed, he took a direct hit from the hot ash.

"Ahhh-hhhh, Jesus, ouch, ouch, ouch. God that's hot," he screamed.

"Careful," I said.

"Son-of-a-bitch, that hurts," He yelled as he slapped at his crotch.

The door flew open a moment later and Mike stepped in. "What the hell's going on in here?" he said. He stood there, holding the door open looking at the two of us.

"He wasn't following the smoking ban and he got burned."

The fat guy had staggered over to the sink and had just taken a handful of water and thrown it onto his jeans.

"That it? You burned yourself?"

"God, that hurts, son-of-a-bitch," he groaned.

Mike shook his head, muttered, "Dumb shit." And left.

People were still chuckling in the bar when I climbed back on the stool next to Louie. He was more than halfway through his drink.

"What the hell was all that?"

"Some idiot was sneaking a cigarette in the can and burned himself."

"Burned himself?"

I gave Louie a look.

"Oh, Jesus. You're kidding."

"No. Let me ask you a question, Louie. I was thinking of this when I was in the can. When we left, I'm pretty sure Manning was going to ask about the sink at Casey's. So I'm guessing he knows about my little altercation with Paris and the hot water."

"Scalding hot water."

"Yeah, whatever. The question is how would he have that information? He either got it from Paris. Or, he got it from someone else who was there."

"Well, you can't be a hundred percent sure he knew anything. It could have just been a lucky guess."

"You believe that?" I said and gave Louie a look.

"No, not really. Probably about a one percent chance of that happening. One more option, Paris could have told someone and maybe they got in touch with Manning or vice-versa."

"Why would he tell anyone?"

"Hey, who knows? Maybe he called your client, Denise…"

"Danielle."

"…and yelled at her. Told her you assaulted him or something. It's not that big a jump to see him trying to grovel and play the sympathy card so he can buy more time. Might be why you can't reach her. Maybe she's frightened or maybe she's worried you'll screw things up even more."

"Yeah, maybe."

"Of course, it may be that he ran into someone and they asked him what the hell happened. Didn't you say he was blistered? I'm guessing there would probably be some discoloration, pink skin, temporary scarring…that sort of thing. It's not a big surprise to see him going into an emergency room somewhere, seeking treatment, maybe prescription burn ointments or something. The folks in the ER ask some questions, he tells the story, maybe drops your name, conveniently. I think they're required to file a report. They'd obviously view the incident as an assault."

That sounded more plausible, Paris using the system to his advantage.

"Course, that suggests he left the place, Casey's at some point and then that sort of suggests it's not him they found there."

"Well, unless he went back, maybe just made a phone call or someone else came to see him there."

I was staring off in the distance, weighing the different options.

"That doesn't address another set of alternatives like maybe someone else entirely was there before, during or after. The place is vacant, but apparently the utilities were still on. Maybe some poor homeless soul was seeking refuge, just wandered in and got caught in the fire. We could sit here all night and not come up with all the possibilities. I'll have another, Mike," Louie said, waving his empty glass.

Mike took his glass, and then looked over at me. "Dev?"

"Yeah sure, why not?"

"However he found out, that damn Manning knows," I said. "God damn it, I could be facing a murder rap here and all I did was tell that jerk Paris that Danielle wanted to be repaid."

"Sounds to me like you better get a handle on where she is and talk to her."

Chapter Twenty-Eight

The first thing I did when I got into the office the following morning was to make some coffee. The second thing I did was to sip coffee and stare out the window at the various working girls catching the bus. Not that my efforts were rewarded, another below zero degree morning with a wind-chill twenty degrees below that. Everyone was so bundled up that with the exception of a bearded guy I couldn't tell if they were men or women. Louie waltzed in around eleven.

"God, it's cold. I just hate this shit. Any coffee left?"

I nodded and set down my binoculars. There was a third story rental unit almost directly across from our office. I had detected some movement between the drawn shade and the window sill and thought I was getting lucky, but the action just turned out to be on a television.

"Any luck?"

"No, I thought one of those two sisters across the way was getting dressed, but it turned out to be the damn TV."

Louie looked at me for a long moment, then shook his head and tossed his suit coat over the back of his chair. He was wearing the same mismatched pinstriped combination from yesterday. His suit coat still had strawberry shake dribbled down the front.

"I meant did you have any luck getting in touch with your client."

"Oh, Danielle, yeah, I'm about to start checking. Hey, I'm guessing you have another suit just like that at home."

He gave me a strange look.

"The stripes, they don't match. The trouser stripes are wider than the ones on your coat."

He looked at the coat then down at his trousers. "Damn it and I was in court this morning."

"I'm sure the strawberry shake you spilled on there served as a distraction."

He chose to ignore my comment. "You better find that client of yours. I'd say the clock is ticking where Manning is concerned and he's not the sort of guy to just dismiss the allegations."

I nodded, sat down and went online.

Most of what I could find online concerning Danielle Roxbury was society column related. She seemed to have been in attendance at every local, big name, fundraising event in town. There were a number of images posted; Danielle looking stunningly beautiful at the Friends of Regions Hospital fundraiser, Danielle sipping champagne at the Friends of the Public Library fundraiser. She was one of twenty sponsors and the best looking of the bunch at a black tie fund raising event for cancer research. There was a shot of her in shorts and a too small T-shirt walking along some lakeside path in support of Breast Cancer Awareness. She'd apparently run a half-marathon in support of St. Paul Public Schools last September. She was decked out in a revealing top, sipping champagne with the public radio crowd. There were a number of mentions of her in attendance at various private clubs, a golf outing or two, more dinners with the high society types. She attended a Thanksgiving high school dance called the Turkey Trot where she appeared as the celebrity chaperone. She graced an opening night gala at the Ordway Theatre a few weeks back for a play I'd never heard of.

I was beginning to get the feeling she had slept with me just to see what life was like on the seamy side of town. Maybe that was why I wasn't getting an answer to the hundreds of phone messages I'd left. It was just that simple. She didn't want to have anything to do with me. Hmm-mmm, not exactly the first time I'd picked up on that type of vibe from a woman.

I decided to check the county tax records. I guessed any mortgage on her home had been free and clear since somewhere back in the Roosevelt administration, that would be Teddy Roosevelt.

Wrong again, at least as far as the Ramsey County tax assessor was concerned. It seemed back taxes had been owed on Danielle Roxbury's inherited mansion for the past three tax periods. That's a year and a half. One would think that at some point over the past eighteen months even a trust fund princess like Danielle would have become aware of an increasing amount of mail from the Ramsey County tax assessor crossing her threshold. She couldn't possibly think that as a member of the privileged class real estate taxes didn't apply to her. Could she?

Renee Paris. I didn't know how, but he was mixed up in this somehow. He had to be. I returned to the online photo album of Danielle sipping champagne with all the right sorts of people at various charity events. I'd just focused on the lovely Danielle when I'd

125

first looked at the images. Now I studied the faces around her.

It didn't take too long. Short, balding, and with just a hint of the rodent on his face, Renee Paris was at the Friends of the Public Library fundraiser. There he was again, standing awfully close behind her and just off to the right at a toney get-together at the Town and Country Club. He was rubbing shoulders with the public radio crowd. Coincidence? Maybe, but a slim one at best. He was a good twenty years older than Danielle and the image of the two of them together looked more like a father-daughter dance photo.

Louie's voice pulled me back to reality.

"Hey, what was that sour faced woman's name yesterday?"

"The lawyer? With Manning? Sinn. Remember, she spelled it, S-I-N-N and then she missed the perfect opportunity for a joke."

"I don't think she was the joking type," Louie said, then clicked his keyboard and waited a few moments.

"Yeah, I thought so. Come over here and check this out. She isn't a lawyer."

An official looking web page was displayed on Louie's screen. It listed Police Department consultants in alphabetical order. The name Sinn, Theobelle ran across the top of Louie's screen next to her less than flattering image. The bio listed her as a department psychologist and profiler.

"What the hell? I thought she was a lawyer. Didn't Manning refer to her as counsel?" I asked.

"Not quite, he referred to her as a consultant. I was so focused on you not saying something stupid his comment just breezed past me."

"That maybe explains the notes she was passing."

"I'm sure she identified you as, well just name it, a pathological liar, a serial killer, a chronic ne'er-do-well, a..."

"I get your point, Louie."

"This puts a little different spin on that damn Manning letting us come down and make a statement. Now I'm really glad we got out of there before he went any further in the direction of that kitchen sink. All the more important to get in touch with your client, that Danielle chick, now."

"Speaking of which, look at what I've got up on my screen."

Louie stepped away from his picnic table desk and over to my computer displaying the Ramsey County tax records.

"That's her address, Danielle's, and she's been in arrears on her real estate taxes for the past eighteen months."

"That's almost to the point where they'll start taking some serious action. They could go as far as seizing the property and selling the place off for back taxes. Eighteen months, hell she's already accrued some pretty hefty fines. The fines might end up being more than the back taxes."

"I don't get it," I said. "Is she that much of a space cadet? She's worth millions. She's got a damn trust fund for Christ's sake. Why would she ignore this? It's not like the tax people are ever going to go away."

"How do you know she's worth millions?"

"Well, that damn house for starters."

"Which is inherited, right?"

"Yeah. But she's got her trust fund?"

"And what do you really know about that? Nothing, except she's the third or fourth generation descending from some robber baron and that's just

127

about the time trust funds start running on empty. She, and the generations before her may have just pissed it all away."

"But she lent that money, fifty grand, to that jerk Renee Paris?"

"So she says. I don't know, maybe it was more of an investment than she let on. Maybe he promised her some huge sort of return. Wouldn't be the first time. Ever hear of Bernie Madoff?"

"You mean the ponzi scheme guy?"

"Yeah, he only dealt with the 'swells' you know the top one percent of the top one percent. The guy swindled all sorts of rich bastards who should have known better. Greed might have come into play with a lot of them. Maybe it's the same thing with your lady friend here."

"Or desperation."

Chapter Twenty-Nine

I was thinking of the online images of Danielle with that schmuck Renee Paris standing in the background. Were they together, a couple? Or was it just an unfortunate coincidence? I wasn't holding too much stock in the coincidence option.

"I've been stuck having to go to a couple of those kind of gigs, most likely they're together," Louie had said when I showed him the images.

I pulled up in front of Danielle's house and phoned her. I let it ring until the answering message kicked in and then hung up. I went through the same routine I'd done before. I climbed out of my car and rang the doorbell. Then I checked the side and rear doors, then the garage. I damn near froze to death again and I still came up with nothing. And, just like before it could be as simple as bad timing with her running out to the grocery store, or not.

I went back to the office and sensed something was wrong the moment I stepped in the door.

"You look like shit," I said.

Louie had a couple of files spread out in front of him and he was clicking keys on his laptop.

"Just looking up a case here. I got a call a while ago from your close personal friend, Detective Manning."

"Manning?"

"'Fraid so. He'd like to see us."

"Oh, shit. What's he want?"

"Seems they've got a tape."

"A tape?"

"Security camera footage, from Casey's, that's all he told me."

I remembered seeing the camera above the back door at Casey's. "About all they're gonna have is me parking and getting out of my car, maybe leaving fifteen minutes later. Nothing I haven't already told them about."

"You sure?"

"Yeah, I saw the camera, it was above the backdoor. I pulled up, got out of my car, pushed a buzzer at the backdoor and Paris let me in. I left maybe fifteen-minutes later. Pretty boring stuff. I'm a little surprised that camera survived the fire. Everything else seemed to be destroyed."

"It didn't have to survive. Those things can be on a digital feed. Whatever they record is probably stored in a cloud or something."

"That's just great," I said. "Okay, let's just go down there and get it over with. I'm continuing to have a real bad feeling on this whole deal and this does nothing to change that."

"If we're gonna go, we should do it now, I've got a court appearance scheduled for three this afternoon."

"I'll drive," I said.

Chapter Thirty

"Right, in here will do just fine, gentlemen," Manning said. I couldn't recall Manning ever referring to me as a gentleman and it made me all the more suspicious.

He ushered us into an industrial sort of room with a flat screen TV mounted on the far wall. There was a low grade covering on the floor that looked to be a half step up from indoor-outdoor carpeting. Hard wooden chairs to squirm on uncomfortably were placed around a sort of industrial gray Formica table. The accommodations were nowhere near as nice as the room we were in yesterday, but it was still a step up from the usual hell-hole I found myself in when talking with Manning.

"Have a seat, fellas." Manning smiled cheerily and I automatically knew I was in deep weeds. The moment we were seated he pressed a couple of buttons on a console and said, "Test one. Test two." Then he played the thing back to make sure it was recording.

I shot a look at Louie who gave a slight wave of his hand, suggesting I shouldn't be worried.

I worried anyway.

"Okay, this is Detective Norris Manning and it's approximately one-thirty-seven…" Manning gave the usual time and place introductions around the room and then smiled.

Louie jumped in immediately. "I'd like to state for the record that Mr. Haskell has volunteered to come down here for a second interview and that we are cooperating fully with your investigation, Detective Manning." Then he sat back with a look suggesting he was waiting to get blind sided.

"So noted," Manning said, sounding just a little too happy for my taste.

"Thank you," Louie said.

"Mr. Haskell, yesterday in our interview…"

"Actually, I'd like to point out that we contacted you and were down here to simply make a statement and participate in any way we could in an effort to further your ongoing investigation." Louie interrupted.

"Of course," Manning said and smiled again.

"Yesterday, during your *statement*, Mr. Haskell, you mentioned discussing with Mr. Renee Paris a matter of some funds believed owed to your client."

Manning paused to look at me and waited until I answered.

"Correct."

"And, you said that you in fact gave that information to Mr. Paris, 'delivered the message' I believe was the term you used. Does that sound correct?"

"Yeah, I'm not really sure on the exact words I may have used, but yes, basically that's what I said."

"You described the kitchen stove. Mr. Paris was apparently cooking on a stove. You mentioned he had a number of large containers bubbling. I think you presumed it was his Bar-B-Que sauce. You mentioned a

132

table with spices, onion skins, garlic, empty tomato containers. Fair to say the usual sorts of things one might expect under the circumstances."

I wasn't sure where Manning was going, so I nodded as I cautiously answered, "Yes."

"You didn't go there to participate in food preparation in any way, did you?"

"No."

"And you didn't go there to participate in any sort of clean up, or packaging or delivery of any finished product, did you, Mr. Haskell?"

"No." Manning had me confused and very wary.

"Of course, like any kitchen operation, you end up making a bit of a mess and I suppose it would have been left to Mr. Paris to clean up, correct? I mean, you certainly didn't feel a need to clean up, did you, Mr. Haskell? You weren't there to assist Mr. Paris in that aspect. Correct?"

"Yes, that is correct," I said and thought *'oh shit.'*

"So, once you delivered your message, once you told Mr. Paris that he owed your client money your job was essentially done. I think that was how you stated it."

Manning waited. I could feel the room getting warmer, the air getting heavier.

"Mr. Haskell? You just left once you delivered your message, as you put it. Correct?"

"Yes, I believe so."

"If you would please direct your attention to the screen. Is this you, Mr. Haskell, leaving Casey's after speaking with Mr. Paris?" Manning pointed to the flat screen and dimed the light as a frozen black and white image projected onto the screen. It was the parking lot behind Casey's. My Lincoln Continental was parked alongside the silver Mercedes, dwarfing the thing.

The image seemed to jump for a half second, the back door to Casey's swung open, but in a jerky sort of way.

"I believe this is the security camera image of you departing, Mr. Haskell. The image is on a delayed feed, a shot taken every couple seconds. That is you, correct?"

"Yes, that's me. And I figured that was Paris' Mercedes. When I got there, pulled in I mean, there was only one set of tire tracks and one set of foot prints in the snow. And the back stoop appeared to have been recently shoveled."

"The set of foot prints you mentioned, where were they?"

I was helping now, we were working together.

"You can't make them out from this angle, but they were on the far side of the Mercedes, on the driver's side. They exited the car and walked to the back door. You can't see it here, but there was a snow shovel leaning against the wall of the building next to the back door and approximately under the security camera. I figured it was probably Paris who shoveled the snow by the back door."

Manning nodded. "You didn't see anyone else around?"

"Nope, no one."

Manning pushed another button and a new image appeared. The Mercedes slowly pulled into view, cutting a path through a good foot of snow. With the sun's reflection off the windshield it was impossible to make out a face. Whoever it was, once they stopped they sat there for a while. It looked like they might be talking on a cell phone. Eventually, the person climbed out of the car. The individual was short and wore a heavy jacket. He had a cap with fur lined ear flaps pulled down on his head. I couldn't be one hundred percent positive, but it looked an awful lot like that rat Paris. He looked back and forth like he was checking the place out before he ventured any further.

"Is that the individual you spoke to?"

"I believe so. It looks like him, except he didn't have that jacket or the fur cap on when I met him. Like I said yesterday, I never met Renee Paris before, but yeah, I'm pretty sure that's the guy I spoke with. Is it actually him, Renee Paris?"

"Yes," Manning said and we all watched as the figure made his jerky, delayed way into the building.

The air didn't feel as heavy as it had a few minutes ago. Maybe I really was helping Manning out and that was all he wanted.

"One more thing, perhaps you could help us with this," Manning said. He punched a button again and then gave a smirk as another image came up on the screen. Judging from the angle of view the camera must have been mounted high up in a corner of the kitchen.

The frozen image displayed Paris standing with his arms folded across his chest. He was leaning back against the table covered with onion skins, empty boxes and spice bottles. To his left and at a ninety-degree angle was the stove with the containers just as I'd described them earlier. The lids sat on top and were pulled halfway off the containers. Across from the stove was the sink. The image was frozen on the screen, but you could make out the steady stream of water flowing from the tap and if you looked closely you could see a cloud of steam rising from the stack of frying pans. Water. Scalding water. A figure with his back to the camera stood across from Paris. There was no doubt that figure was me.

"Let's just see what happens here, shall we?" Manning said and then put the image in motion, not waiting for my answer.

There wasn't any audio, thank God. But even in the every-few-second intervals the jerky film left no question as to what was happening. Paris's head appeared to take a harder whack than I realized when I kicked his feet out from underneath him and he caught the edge of the table as he went down. I had him yanked off the floor and marching across the room toward the sink almost immediately. Then I slammed him into the edge of the sink and his legs sort of flew out from beneath him.

When it showed me thrusting his head into the scalding tap water I caught myself rubbing my hands protectively beneath the table. Even though there wasn't any sound, I could hear him screaming. Then, just to top off our little love dance, he was down on the ground looking like he was gasping for life when I back handed him with the aluminum frying pan. He had been threatening to sue me at that point of our discussion, but on the jerking security tape it looked like he was pleading for mercy. We didn't need any sound here either. I think all of us heard the dull 'thunk' as I bounced the large frying pan off thick skull.

Manning froze the image of a dazed Renee Paris looking frightened out of his wits while I lorded over him with a frying pan.

"Well, I don't know. I guess like you said, Mr. Haskell, you were just there to deliver a message. Right?"

Chapter Thirty-One

"Come on, Louie, cut me some slack. Do you really think I would have done that if I knew there was a God damn security camera filming everything?"

"Don't even go there. The fact of the matter is you did it. You assaulted the bastard and Manning's got the entire thing on that security tape. Christ, you're lucky YouTube hasn't gotten hold of the thing and it went viral, out there for everyone to see."

We were driving back to the office. Manning had given me possibly the coldest smile I'd ever seen followed up with, "I'm sure we'll be in touch," as we departed.

"And another thing, thanks for eliminating the twin brother defense. Claiming you were the only other individual there. Reminding Manning about the *one* set of footprints, the *one* set of tire tracks," Louie said.

"I thought I was helping."

"Jesus Christ, ever hear of the Stockholm syndrome? You were helping all right, Dev. Helping Manning build his case against you."

"You were really thinking of using that, the twin brother thing?"

"It may have been our best option. It's a half-step up from pleading someone's an orphan after they murdered their parents. Look, like I may have suggested before, the damn clock's ticking. Manning is just getting all his facts lined up until he has an airtight case against you. Once he gets a confirmation on who was roasted in that fire he'll be coming for you. Today's little academy award presentation makes you suspect numero uno."

"Shit."

"You can say that again."

"Shit."

Louie looked at me, shook his head and said, "I gotta be in court in forty minutes. I'm pleading for an alternative treatment sentence instead of incarceration for a DUI defendant. Once I'm finished with that you're buying the drinks."

"You can't be thinking of celebrating after what just transpired."

"You kidding? God, no. We're gonna start planning."

Chapter Thirty-Two

About all we came up with in our planning session was a hefty bar tab that I got stuck with. Oh, and Louie's cab fare home.

I, on the other hand had the brilliant, alcohol fueled idea to drive past Danielle's house. Just to see if there might be a light on in the place after two in the morning. There wasn't. But, there was someone on my ass as I drove home. I'd been drinking with Louie which was almost the same thing as binge drinking. I made two different turns down side streets and the headlights still followed right behind me. They may have dropped back a bit, but they were still there. I figured I had enough on my plate and didn't need to be stopped for driving under the influence, so I pulled over to the curb on Portland Avenue and got out of my car.

I walked down two doors and then up the set of front steps like I was going to the house. The headlights drove past and I pretended not to notice. I watched the car fade down the street, some non-descript gray thing. I waited while it continued out of sight. I was freezing by the time the thing disappeared and I rushed back to my car only to realize that in my haste I'd left my keys in the ignition and locked the door.

I was maybe a good half-mile from home and had no other option but to head in that direction. It was possibly the coldest seven or eight minutes of my life. I couldn't feel my fingers or my feet by the time I arrived at my place. My face was numb and my ears were so cold they'd stopped hurting three blocks back. The cold had made me dreadfully sober. Then, just to make things perfect, I had to dig through about two feet of snow, looking for the fake rock where I hid my spare house key. I found the damn thing, but it had taken another five minutes. I couldn't stop shivering once I got inside so I ran a hot shower and stood underneath it for the better part of forty minutes. I tossed an extra quilt and a heavy wool coat over the down comforter on my bed and then crawled underneath.

When I woke the following morning my hands and feet still hurt and the skin on my ears and cheeks looked burned, frost bite.

Chapter Thirty-Three

This morning the temperature had risen five degrees, to a balmy minus twenty-six on the Fahrenheit scale. I got dressed and then dug out some skin cream that a former girlfriend had left behind. The stuff was sort of purple tinted and lavender scented, but I slathered it on my face and ears anyway. I didn't plan on walking and I figured a taxi over to my car would run me at least ten bucks, so I phoned Heidi.

"Well, Dev. Gee, a call first thing in the morning. It's either gotta be bail money, by the way my answer is still *no*. Or, you want me to pick up some groceries so you don't have to venture outside, in which case the answer is the same, no."

"Good morning, Heidi. As a matter of fact, wrong on both counts. Look, if you don't have anything going on, I had an appointment cancel and I just wanted to see about taking you out for breakfast, that's all."

"Really?" She didn't sound convinced.

"Yeah, look, no problem if you're busy. I was just thinking it would be nice to maybe chat and…"

"Chat?"

"Yeah."

"You're sure you're not in jail?"

141

"No. I mean, yes, I'm sure I'm not in jail. Look, if you can join me, you pick the place."

"Really? You're not thinking your usual dreadfully sleazy fast-food, greasy diner sort of place?"

"Honest. You pick."

"The White Hen? You know how I just love that place."

"Perfect, meet you there in twenty?"

"Gee, thanks Dev, see you there."

She sounded all excited. I figured that was the place she'd pick. I could almost see it from my front door. I'd buy her breakfast and then have her give me a ride back to my car. I stuffed a spare car key in my pocket and headed out the door.

Heidi ordered some sort of calorie-free vegan side dish that came with weak tea. I was famished after almost freezing to death on my walk home the night before and ordered eggs Benedict with extra hollandaise sauce, a side of blueberry pancakes and a side of bacon.

"Hey, can I ask you something about the other morning when I drove you back to Bunnies?"

"What? So that's what this was about. I knew you acting nice was too good to be true. No, Dev, you're not going to ride me after breakfast so just stop right there. Honest to God, sometimes I just can't believe you. You're never satisfied, you just…"

"Heidi, calm down. That's not what I was going to say."

"Oh, really?"

"Yes, really. What I wanted to ask you about was my phone number that was supposed to be in the ladies room at Bunnies."

"Yeah, we already covered this. I told you it wasn't there, we all went in and looked."

"The woman who called me might have been a little over served."

"There's a surprise."

"Can I finish here? Maybe it wasn't on the door of the bathroom stall. I'm thinking she might have made a mistake and it was on a wall or by the mirror or something."

"Hmmm-mmm, great idea, except that there were five of us and we looked all over the place. We really wanted to find it. I told you Karen was going to take a picture with her phone and post it on Facebook."

"She was going to post my phone number on Facebook? What the hell?"

"Oh, yeah, I forgot, business is so good you don't need the advertising. Besides relax, like I said it wasn't there."

"And you don't think it could have been wiped off when they were cleaning?"

"Cleaning? Are you kidding? We're lucky they have toilet paper in there."

She was picking at some spinach leaves with her fork when I pushed away my empty eggs Benedict platter and started in on the blueberry pancakes.

"How can you eat all that? The cholesterol alone will probably give you a massive coronary."

"I've been walking and it works up an appetite."

"Walking? You? Yeah right, sure you have. When?"

"Just last night as a matter of fact."

"Last night? Get out of here. It was about minus forty with the wind chill."

"You're telling me. Actually, I locked my keys in the car and had to walk home. Damn near froze to death."

"You walked home? From where? The Spot?"

143

"No, actually not too far from here. Well, probably a mile or two. I'm heading back that way once we finish."

"Dev, it's still about minus twenty out there. Let me give you a ride."

"Oh, you don't have to do that."

"You just bought breakfast, it's the least I can do."

"You sure?"

"I insist, now not another word."

Heidi's breakfast ran seven bucks so I considered myself three dollars ahead of the game.

As we pulled away from the White Hen, she said, "Buckle up, and are you wearing perfume or something?"

"No. Oh, you know what? I think I actually got some minor frost bite last night walking home so I put some cream on my face this morning. The stuff was lavender scented."

She shot me a look like she didn't believe me.

"Honest. Hey, take a right on Portland, my car is up there a mile or two."

Once she turned I could see my car at the far end of the block.

"Is that it just up there?" Heidi asked.

"Yeah, hmmm-mmm, it seemed a lot further last night. Probably the cold."

As we pulled alongside I spotted a parking ticket on my windshield.

"Naughty, naughty." Heidi laughed.

"Are you kidding me? This is like the second one in about two weeks."

"I know, what were they thinking? Imagine making you follow the same parking restrictions the rest of us have to abide by."

"Whatever. Thanks for the ride."

She just laughed at me as I got out and then drove away. The Lincoln slowly groaned to life. I knew the feeling in this weather. I debated about going to the office or back to bed. Surprisingly, I opted for the responsible move.

Chapter Thirty-Four

"I was beginning to wonder if you were gonna show up or just stay in bed. I left some coffee for you," Louie said.

He was seated at his picnic table and didn't look up. A number of files were haphazardly spread out in front of him and he was furiously tapping keys on his laptop. He was wearing his jacket and a wool cap emblazoned with a green shamrock. 'Ireland' surrounded the shamrock in gold letters.

"You just in?"

"No, it's so damn cold I'm still freezing. You can feel the cold coming right through that window, another polar vortex according to the weather guy, whatever the hell that is. God, I hate this shit."

"Tell me about it, I had to walk home last night."

"From The Spot?"

"No, I was checking on something then thought a car was following me. I was afraid it might be the cops." I went on to tell Louie about locking the keys in my car, breakfast with Heidi, and the parking ticket.

He shook his head and then said, "You better get your ducks in a row. Manning's got you at the scene. He's got you assaulting Renee Paris. He's got your

146

statement about 'delivering a message'. Christ, he'll probably have the prosecution open with that line. You've got to find your client, this Danielle woman, Dev, and find her soon."

"I'm trying to, that's who I was checking on last night. Not that it did any good."

As if on cue an unknown number rang my phone. *'Ting-A-Ling.'*

"I don't believe it," I said and answered. "Haskell Investigations."

"Dev. Danielle. I thought our deal was you were going to check in with me every day."

"That's what I've been doing, Danielle. Checking in every day, you just never answer. Did you get any of my messages?"

"No. What number are you calling?"

I told her the number.

"Oh. I'm using a different phone, new number," she said like it was no big deal.

"I even went over and checked out your house."

"You did? When?"

"A couple of times. I walked all around the place, checked the side door and your garage. I even drove past late last night as a matter of fact."

"Oh, so those were your footprints we saw in the snow the other day? That was you who walked along the side yard, in the back and all around the garage?"

I caught the 'we', but just filed it away and didn't ask. "Yeah, like I said, I've been over there checking out the place."

"God, I wish you would have told me. I didn't know what to think. I thought someone was trying to break in, for God's sake. You know how big this place is. This kind of weather everything is creaking and

147

cracking in the middle of the night. Those footprints you left scared me half to death."

I ignored her rant and asked, "Did you hear anything from Renee Paris?"

"No, not so much as a text message. I don't know what my next step will be."

"I still think your best bet is to get an attorney and take him to court."

"I suppose, I just don't know."

"You're aware that the place where I met him, Casey's, burned down?"

"Well, I heard the news report a few days ago. I don't get the paper anymore. But that has nothing to do with me."

"I know it doesn't, Danielle which is exactly why I went down to the police station and made a statement."

"A statement?" she half shouted.

"Yeah, just in case someone saw me or my car there. I wanted the cops to know I'd been there, that I spoke with Paris and when I left everything seemed just fine." I didn't see any point in mentioning the security tapes to her.

"What did they say?"

"Not much. I didn't expect them to, actually. I just wanted to get it on the record. Well and then help their investigation anyway I can."

"They hired you?" She sounded concerned.

"No. I meant if they had any questions, anything I might be able to answer or confirm I wanted them to feel comfortable getting in touch with me." I thought, *'Yeah, that's what I wanted, Manning feeling comfortable.'* I picked up on the look Louie was giving me.

"Did you tell them about me?" Suddenly there was an edge to her voice.

"No of course not, but listen, Danielle, I wondered in the interest of full disclosure and helping their investigation would you mind if I gave them your name? I'd like to let them know you were the client that asked me to contact Paris. Get it on the record that neither one of us is hiding anything."

"I'm not hiding anything. I told you I haven't seen Renee since…well, since forever. You sure you didn't tell the police my name?"

"I didn't. That's why I'm asking you now. I wanted to make sure it was all right with you before I passed your name on. They'll find out sooner or later. Your name is bound to be listed along with maybe a thousand other people who were involved with Paris. It would just be a good idea to get it out there on your terms before the police come around knocking. And believe me, they will, come around knocking, that is."

"You think they'll want to talk to me? The police?" Her voice had raised an octave.

"I don't know, Danielle, maybe, maybe not. I'm just saying you could do yourself a favor by letting them know. Obviously your concern about being repaid was one of, if not the last thing, presented to Paris before that fire. You saw the report about human remains being found in the rubble, didn't you?"

"I didn't have anything to do with that." She sounded defensive as she half-yelled.

"I'm not saying you did, Danielle. I'm just suggesting that in your own interest it would probably make sense to let them know you have nothing to hide."

"I don't have anything to hide."

"Exactly, which is why you should get in touch with them or let me tell them you were the client I was working for when I spoke with Paris." It was beginning to feel like I was talking to a petulant thirteen-year-old.

"I'm just not sure. I'll have to think about it."

"Well, do what you want. Just remember, they aren't going to be sitting around waiting. Sooner or later you'll have to move on this, and the sooner you do, the better it will be."

"Okay, okay. I get it. I just don't like being pressured, is all."

"Believe me, this is nothing like the pressure the police can put you under. You may want to talk to your attorney first. See what they suggest. I'm not trying to pressure you, Danielle, honest. I'm just giving you a heads up."

"Okay, okay, God, I already told you, I'll think about it." She sounded like a snippy little teenager.

"Fine, just don't think too long. I gotta believe the police are working on this full time. If the remains they found turn out to be Paris they are going to zero in on you and me."

"Well, then it sounds like we should probably end our working relationship." She spoke in almost a pouty, little girl way, as if to say, *'I'll show you.'*

"Our working relationship?"

"Well, yes. I mean, I enjoyed everything and all, but I'm feeling like you've done as much as you can. And, well, maybe it would just be better if we weren't in touch any longer. I mean, you did talk to him, Renee, and I haven't heard back, so obviously that didn't work. I think the next thing I should do is maybe just take your advice."

"My advice?" Either she wasn't catching on or she was suddenly way ahead of me, I wasn't sure which it was.

"Yeah, I'll just get in touch with my family's attorney and take Renee to court. I don't know, maybe it was a mistake to hire you in the first place."

150

"To hire me? Danielle, it's not like I forced you. Remember? You called me. It was the middle of the night, I was asleep and you were sitting on the toilet at Bun..."

"I think I'll just contact my attorney. I should have done that in the first place instead of letting you get involved and creating this horrible mess."

"Horrible mess?"

"Whatever. Look, I can't thank you enough for *everything* you've done," she said and hung up.

I called her back once I calmed down. I got a message that said, "The person at this number is not taking calls at this time."

"So?" Louie asked after I'd hung up.

"So nothing. Apparently, everything is suddenly my fault. She's going to contact her family attorney. Then I think she fired me. I don't know it's almost like she's living in her own little dream world."

"Gee, there's a surprise someone with a trust fund not dealing with reality. Did she happen to mention who her attorney is?"

"No, and I think it might make a lot of sense to not try and grab her as a client, if that's the direction you're heading."

"Believe me I don't need her kind of business. Like I said, reality isn't the strong suit."

"What a strange chick. Hey, speaking of attorneys, does this name ring a bell with you? Richard Hedstrom?"

"God, you're kidding? The Dick Head? Where did you run into that jackass?"

"Actually, I didn't. A pal of mine had used him sometime back. His wife mentioned the guy's name. I'd never heard of him before."

151

"I think he was a couple years ahead of me in law school. Not the kind of guy who's easy to like, if you know what I mean."

"I'm not sure I do."

"I don't know exactly. It's not that he's an intentional jerk or anything. It just always seems to work out that way. He's all about himself and if you get screwed in the process, well, that wasn't his intention, so it's not his fault. He's another one of those people who really doesn't need anyone else. He's just perfectly content with himself. My guess, your pal feels he got screwed. The truth is whenever anyone deals with guys like the Dick Head, you're just never going to come out on top."

"Sounds like Renee Paris."

"I guess it does now that you mention it. Maybe birds of a feather."

"This gal, my friend's wife, she thinks Hedstrom is tied into Renee Paris, somehow."

"Let me guess, Dick Head was their attorney, he was going to file an action or a cease and desist order or something against Paris and they're out a couple of grand and little or nothing to show for it."

"Close. Actually, they're out ten grand, cash up front, with nothing to show for it. I forget how or maybe she never even told me. But she seemed pretty sure Hedstrom and Paris were tied in together."

"Possibly, from the sounds of it. Obviously they'd swim in the same shitty water, developers and bankers. Not to defend Hedstrom, but your friends may not have had much of a case to begin with. A lot of people end up thinking they got screwed by their attorney because when the deal was cut they were too smart and too special, so they didn't need an attorney in the first place. They somehow get it in their heads that they don't have to read the fine print like the rest of us."

"I don't know."

"That cash up front she referred to, Dick Head probably called it a retainer, he may've known going in that they didn't have much of a shot. He may have even tried to talk them out of the whole undertaking. You'd be surprised the hours a guy can spend filing briefs, working a case and after you give it your very best effort, the client doesn't think he should have to pay. All because you weren't successful and couldn't grab his one percent shot at victory."

"Yeah, she may have alluded to some of that, at least the too smart angle when dealing with Paris," I said.

"Neither one of them, Paris or Hedstrom would seem to be the sort of person you could count on to watch your back. If they're working together, Paris and Hedstrom, everyone else is going to come out on the short end of the stick. That's just an unpleasant fact of life."

"I think she knows that now."

"Wow, Richie Hedstrom, the Dick Head. Man, I haven't thought of him in years."

Chapter Thirty-Five

I knew I should be relieved, but it bothered me that Danielle had fired me. Even though I'd done exactly what she asked, and for all intents and purposes I'd successfully completed my task. I decided not to let her actions bother me. I simply moved beyond her stupid, petty, childish, rash, unimportant, and inconsequential outburst and went in a completely different direction. I wanted to find out everything I could regarding Richard Hedstrom.

I went online to check him out. He looked squeaky clean at least as far as his Google persona read. There were a couple of articles where his name was mentioned, but nothing earth shattering. Like Louie, he seemed to have developed a specialized law practice. The only difference was Hedstrom dealt with commercial development instead of drink related cases. That put him in the same cess pool with the likes of Renee Paris, but it also put him in with good guys like Jimmy White. Hey, there were even sleaze balls in my business.

A reverse directory search gave his address as living in a pretty tony condo along the river. Like sixty-percent of today's population it didn't list a land line

154

phone number. It didn't list the names of any other individuals at the address, either. No wife or kids which meant, there was a fifty-fifty chance, maybe, that he lived alone.

I knew the development. There were five, four story brick buildings with underground parking, tree lined brick paths and flower gardens along the river. They were situated on a rise along a bend in the Mississippi, where every unit boasted a balcony with a view of the river. The entire area was cordoned off from average people like me by thick hedges and a manned guard house that gave you clearance before you could drive in.

No casual callers here, the guards had to be alerted in advance of your arrival and departure times. They made a note of who you were, and probably took your picture and finger prints before they issued you a parking permit that had to be placed on the dash of your car. The condo units started at about nine hundred and fifty grand and headed north depending on amenities. They were populated by heavy hitters and the 'Swells'. The development was named River View Terrace, but collectively referred to around town as the *'Viagra Triangle'*.

I'd been in there once, about six years ago, attending an anniversary celebration of a girlfriend's parents. She dumped me the following morning on her way out the door. I hadn't been invited back since.

"I'm sorry, sir. I don't seem to find your name on the list. As a matter of fact, I don't see any appointments scheduled for Mr. Hedstrom for the entire afternoon." The guard spoke to me via a speaker. He appeared comfortable, seated in his cushioned black chair where he looked down on me from inside his heated guard shack. He flipped through pages on his

155

clip board and searched for my name that wasn't there. He wore a black sweater with epaulets and some sort of official looking badge embroidered over his left breast. A mug of coffee steamed on the counter in front of him.

I was freezing behind the wheel of my Lincoln. The heater was apparently in one of its temperamental moods and not performing. I had the window rolled down so I could talk to the guard. Something close to a gale force wind was blowing off the frozen Mississippi, into my car and whipping trash and an old newspaper around the back seat. I was sure he could hear my teeth chattering as I spoke.

"I just talked with him less than twenty minutes ago. He said he was going to jump in the shower. I've got a business meeting scheduled with him at two."

At the mention of a business meeting the guard's eyes darted sideways for a moment, making note of the Lincoln. He looked down at me questioningly from his heated perch inside the guard shack. From where he sat he could no doubt catch the trash blowing around in my back seat.

"Like I said before, sir. I don't have you listed on our arrival directory. I'm terribly sorry, but it is our policy."

I glanced in the rear view mirror and what looked like a shiny new Range Rover had just turned off Shepard Road and was heading toward us. The guard glanced behind me at the same time and seemed to make a mental note.

"I wonder. Could you call him and check? I would, but my phone isn't getting any service down here, must be those bluffs behind us." I smiled.

He gave a long stare that delivered his message, and then glanced at the Range Rover now idling behind me. There was a woman sitting behind the wheel who looked to be in her twenties. From what I could determine in my rearview mirror her matching hat and fur coat were probably worth more than my Lincoln. I watched as she took the moment to lower her sun visor and she began to apply makeup in the mirror. The guard caught it too then reluctantly reached for his phone.

As he waited listening to the phone ringing on the other end his scowl deepened. "Sorry, sir, no answer."

"Must still be in the shower. What number did you call? He's got a couple of phones," I said, making it up as I went along.

The guard closed his eyes for a long moment probably pleading to God to give him strength. He glanced at his clip board and rattled off a number.

"That's six-five-one area code, right?"

"Yes it is. Sir, I'm very sorry, but I'm going to have to ask you to pull around and find some place where your phone works. Call Mr. Hedstrom and have him get in touch with us. Then I'd be happy to admit you."

"I understand. Thanks for your help," I said and began to pull around the guard shack. The Lincoln sort of farted and emitted a cloud of black exhaust that withstood the gale force for a long moment before contaminating the formerly pristine snow. All the while I was repeating the phone number to myself. The Lincoln was so long I had to pull ahead at an angle, back up and pull ahead for a few more feet then back up again to complete my U-turn.

As I backed up I looked at the gorgeous blonde behind the wheel of the Range Rover. She lowered her window, handed the guard an envelope and said, "Hi, Gerry."

Gerry pocketed the envelope and said something back. She glanced in my direction and smiled. Just as I pulled ahead I heard her say, "No problem, it happens."

By the time I made it around the guard shack and headed back out to Shepard Road the Range Rover had already driven into the complex. I remembered the place was called the Viagra Triangle and wondered if she was working.

Chapter Thirty-Six

I took the first exit off Shepard road, drove up a hill and pulled into the Irving Park neighborhood. I was just a block from the historic Ramsey House, home to Minnesota's first governor. I parked across from a little park with a frozen water fountain and dialed the number the guard had given me. I continued to repeat the number out loud as I dialed.

The phone rang a half dozen times before a recording came on that said, "The message center you have reached is full at this time."

Apparently Dick Head didn't feel the need to answer his phone or check his messages.

The heater in the Lincoln was sputtering, threatening to spring to life and I decided to take a drive past Danielle's home. That quickly turned out to be a disappointing waste of my time and I drove back to the office. On the way, the heater alternated between blowing a semblance of heat or pungent exhaust fumes into the car. I had to crack open the driver's window for some fresh air just to keep me from being asphyxiated. I parked right in front of our building and ran inside.

It was after three, and I smelled the empty coffee pot burning the moment I unlocked the door. Louie was nowhere around. I turned the coffee off then sat at my desk with my jacket on, starring out the window, thinking. Louie drifted in about four-thirty.

"What smells?"

"You left the coffee pot on, again."

"Oh," he said, and tossed his briefcase on the picnic table.

"Not 'oh', Louie. You're going to burn the place down one of these days."

"Hey, I'm not the only one. You've done it too."

"No argument, but you seem to be doing it a lot more often. I don't know, I suppose we could just put a timer on that outlet so the thing shuts off by noon every day."

"Sounds like a real pain," Louie said.

"How about a better idea, we pool our resources, fifteen bucks a pop and for thirty bucks we buy a new coffee maker that automatically shuts off after an hour or two," I said.

"That seems to make more sense. I need to go over to The Spot anyway. I'll get some cash. You game?"

"You buying?" I asked.

"Apparently."

We weren't in there long, at least not by our standards. Louie told me about the case he lost that afternoon, a client of his up on a fourth DUI in five years. Louie tried to get him sentenced to in-patient treatment, but since that hadn't worked the last two times the guy drew four years.

"How'd your day go?" he asked, then drained his glass and signaled for another by pushing his empty toward the back edge of the bar.

"About the same, only no one drew jail time. You heard me talking to Princess Danielle this morning and getting fired. Things sort of drifted downhill from there.

160

I tried to get Richard Hedstrom's phone number from the guard shack down at the Viagra Triangle."

"Those ritzy condos on the river? He's got a place down there?"

"Yep. I made like I had an appointment to see him, but the bastards wouldn't let me in, and gave me his phone number to call instead."

"Nice security."

"Well, that's the short version."

Louie nodded then sipped from the fresh pour Mike had just placed in front of him.

"I called the number they gave me, but it dropped me into one of those recordings about the message center being full. Either he doesn't check his messages, he's been somewhere out of range for awhile, or the thing is broken."

Louie shook his head. "Maybe he's on vacation, but a guy with his kind of practice is on call twenty-four-seven. He could be sitting on a beach in Hawaii, but if he was needed, he'd have to hop on the next flight back here. His clients are flush enough. They don't get that kind of service, they'll drop Dick Head like a hot potato."

"Good point. I don't know there's just something about this whole deal that bugs me."

"Take a bit of advice from a pal?" Louie said then looked at me over the rim of his glass.

I nodded.

"You did your bit and then got a quick glimpse of la-la land from that Danielle chick this morning. Take that for what it's worth. Her reaction was to not take your advice even though you told her a much better way to deal with the situation. Plan B, having you tell Paris he owed her money didn't work. No surprise there. Her way of dealing with that is to blame you.

161

She's never had to work for anything, she most likely never will, and she's never made a mistake, just ask her. You need to do two things. First, consider it a profitable little venture that you are thankfully finished with. Then second, move on. As awful as it may sound, you should call your buddy at that insurance company and see if he has more files you can check references on."

"Oh, God, talk about a long day."

"Yeah, that you got paid for while you sat in the comfort of the office making an occasional phone call. In between times you could continue to leer at women out on the street. Oh, and not have to worry about the likes of Detective Norris Manning."

"Don't confuse me with the facts," I said and climbed off my stool.

"Hey, come on, I'll buy a round, it's my turn," Louie said.

"You're right it is. In fact, it's way past your turn, but I'm heading home. I'll see you in the morning," I said and threw some cash on the bar.

"You're not pissed off, are you?"

"No, sage advice, Louie thanks. I get it. I'm just gonna head home and watch a flick or something. But I'll take a rain check on that drink, pal."

"Suit yourself," Louie said, then drained his glass and signaled Mike for another refill.

I pulled my gloves on as I went out the door. God, it was cold. This damn polar vortex thing could leave the region anytime and it would be okay with me. At this hour of the night traffic was usually heavy enough that you could see a headlight or two coming toward you in either direction. Tonight, there was nothing, the streets were quiet. One car was idling across the street and up a half-dozen doors behind my Lincoln. I figured the owner would run out the door and jump in once the car was warm. Other than an idling vehicle, it was dead on the street. I guessed everyone was doing what I was about to do. Hunker down under a fleece blanket in front of the TV.

I crossed the intersection at an angle, against the red light, not that it made any difference without anyone on the road. I pulled my collar up, hunched my shoulders and wished I'd worn a cap. I exhaled inside my jacket, hoping my breath would keep me warm. I prayed the heater would work in the Lincoln on the way home.

I pulled a glove off and fished the car keys out of my jacket pocket. The cold air was hurting my hand and I half trotted toward the Lincoln. The car halfway up the block pulled away from the curb and started down the street. I heard the engine accelerate as it came toward me. I could tell by the sound of the engine the vehicle was picking up a lot of speed as the sound from the engine whined higher and higher. I looked up and the guy hadn't switched his headlights on.

I waved my arm to signal I was standing out in the street as I started to open the car door, expecting the vehicle to veer toward the center of the road. It didn't. Instead, it zeroed in on me and the pitch of the engine suddenly sounded like the guy had floored it.

It was one of those nano-second decisions that seem to move in slow motion. There wasn't time to make it inside the Lincoln. I let go of the door, hopped a step or two and dove head first over the hood just as the vehicle side swiped the Lincoln. Fear is a powerful motivator. I was in mid-air going over the far side of the hood when the Lincoln caught me at about the knees and spun me up and around in mid-air. I sort of turned and bounced off the trunk of the Lincoln as it

163

shot past me, then landed behind the thing half in the street. I was vaguely aware of taillights lighting up and then quickly fading from view.

Chapter Thirty-Seven

"Are you kidding? No, Mr. Romantic over there took me to a nude beach with a pitcher of margaritas which he proceeded to drink while he told me he didn't need sun screen. He got so sun-burned I couldn't touch him for the rest of the trip."

My eyes were closed, but I knew it was Heidi's voice. The laughter sounded maybe like Louie and some women I didn't recognize.

"They always think they know better." One of the women chuckled.

I slowly opened my eyes and looked around. The walls in the room were some sort of off-white. There was a steel track in the ceiling with a curtain hanging from it. Apparently I was in a hospital bed, and it looked like I was attached to some sort of monitor. I wiggled my toes and then my fingers. I moved my head slowly from side to side.

As I slowly raised my knees a voice said, "Well, look who's come around. How are we doing, Mr. Haskell?" A nurse walked into view and looked me over. She was older than me, with salt and pepper hair in a short sort of bob cut. As she spoke she adjusted the stethoscope from around her neck and laid it on my chest.

"What the hell happened?"

"Just a minute, please. Okay?" she said not really asking for my permission. She waited a long moment, then placed the stethoscope against my neck and turned her wrist to check her watch.

"Where…"

"Almost finished here." Then another long moment as she continued to stare at her watch. "Now," she said, then pulled the stethoscope out of her ears and let it hang around her neck. She held up her hand and raised the index finger. Her fingernail was neatly trimmed and polish free. "How many fingers?"

"One."

"Good, you can count. Now, follow my finger with your eyes. Don't turn your head. No, I said don't turn your head. Yes, that's it, much better and up and down and back, yes and forth, yes. How are we feeling?"

I did a quick assessment. "I think okay. Maybe a little banged up on my right side. My elbows hurt, but I can bend them." And then did.

"You're a lucky man, Mr. Haskell."

Her nametag read E. Bauer. I wondered if she was possibly related to Heidi?

"Must have been a drunk driver," Louie chirped in from the back of the room.

"You doing okay, Dev?" Heidi asked and stepped into view.

"I think I've had sunburns that were worse," I said.

"Oh, so you remember Puerto Vallarta?" Heidi said and stood behind the nurse.

Everyone sort of chuckled.

"I'll alert our consultant. I'd say he'll be going home early this afternoon," the nurse said to Heidi.

166

"Thanks, Eve, you've been great," Heidi said and gave her a kiss on the cheek.

"We're just happy to get him out of here." The nurse chuckled. "Give my best to your Mom," she said and left the room with a younger nurse in tow.

"Louie, go back to the office and get my…"

"Stop right there, Mister. You're not in charge here," Heidi said. "Louie, I'll give you a call once I get him home. It might be hours before we're released here. No sense in everyone wasting their time. I'm going down to the cafeteria and get a yogurt and some fruit for you, Dev. I'll be back in a few minutes."

"Bacon and some pancakes would be better," I said.

"I don't think so. I'll call you when he's home," she said to Louie and marched off in the direction of the cafeteria.

Louie waited a long minute after the door closed. Then he cautiously approached my bed. "What the hell happened, Dev? It couldn't have been more than sixty seconds from when you left The Spot. Some drunk driver?"

"You mean one of your clients?" I half joked, but cut off my chuckle as a wave of pain stabbed across my chest.

"I don't know, maybe. Just glad you're okay. Sorry to say, I think your car is probably toast."

"The Lincoln?"

"What's left of it. A good portion of the driver's side is torn off. The door was out in the intersection. The force of the collision pushed your car into the concrete bus bench, so your radiator and engine were kind of where the front seat used to be. Windshield's gone."

167

"That wasn't any drunk driver, Louie. That car was waiting for me when I came out of The Spot."

"Waiting for you?"

"There wasn't a car on the street last night when I left. I saw this car parked at the curb halfway up the block, engine running. Figured they were just warming up or something. Next thing I know the damn car takes off and comes barreling down the street, heading directly for me with its lights off."

"Didn't they see you?"

"That's what I'm saying, they did see me. They tried to run me down. Tried to kill me."

"Kill you? God, then you're awfully damn lucky, Dev."

"Maybe."

"Any idea who? Or why? Was it someone's husband?"

"No to your first two questions and I don't think so to your third," I said.

Heidi strolled back into the room. "Okay, enough business, boys. Nothing that can't wait. Louie, go do something productive. Dev, here, start to eat healthy. I got a yogurt and here's a cranberry juice for you, it will help keep you hydrated."

"What do you have?" I asked. Heidi was holding a small white Styrofoam carton in her left hand behind her back as discreetly as possible.

"You know I just love cinnamon rolls," she said.

"Yeah, I know that. So do I. You didn't get me one?"

"Don't start, Dev. Louie, don't you have something you should be doing?"

"I got a court appearance at one. Dev, it shouldn't go longer than twenty or thirty minutes. Give me a call when you're ready to talk."

168

"Thanks, Louie," I said.

"Bye, Louie, thank you," Heidi said through a mouthful of cinnamon roll.

Chapter Thirty-Eight

"**God, thanks for bringing** this," I said and took another bite of my pizza slice.

"No problemo," Louie said. "I never knew your pal Heidi was into the whole health food kick."

"Believe me, she isn't. She just did that to yank my chain and lord it over me. Thank God she had a meeting this afternoon. I was afraid she was gonna make me go outside for a walk."

"It's fifteen below, Dev."

"Yeah, she would have just chalked that up to fresh air. I did get her to drive me past the office on the way home, just to see if I could figure anything out."

"And?"

"Other than the wrecked bus stop bench and some glass on the street, there wasn't that much to see."

"Yeah, your deal happened maybe about eight last night. I'll bet everything was cleaned up and hauled away before eleven. Paramedics had you out of there before the second squad car made it to the scene. You are just so damn lucky, Dev. This could have been a hell of a lot worse."

"You kidding? The Lincoln's totaled."

"Yeah, and you're here to tell the story, so shut up. I've been thinking about what you said earlier, that they were waiting for you. Any ideas who?"

"Not really. When Heidi drove me past I think I figured out where that car was waiting. I was guessing a half dozen doors up the block, I actually counted eight."

"If that's the case that they were waiting for you, you're damn lucky they didn't catch you out in the open."

"Yeah. I don't know, maybe they didn't recognize me at first. Maybe they were asleep or screwing with the radio. Anyway, a couple of seconds earlier and they would have caught me just standing there in the middle of the intersection."

"And no one comes to mind?"

"A long shot, Paris."

"That's pretty thin. I'm still thinking there's an awfully good chance he was roasted in that fire at Casey's."

"Yeah, me too."

"What about your former employer?"

I gave Louie a blank look.

"The princess, that Danielle Roxbury," he said, then stuffed the rest of a pizza slice into his mouth.

"She's definitely looney enough, but I can't see her actually getting her hands dirty and doing it, let alone having the ability to effectively flee the scene. If it had been her she'd have done something completely psycho, like backing up and coming at me again. Then she'd get out of the car, say she was sorry and ask if I was all right."

"Maybe she hired someone."

"Yeah, but it would have been on short notice. I don't know. Would she have a contact like that? Maybe. I couldn't determine what kind of car it was,

171

other than black or maybe dark green or blue. It did seem to be a newer model and not some old beater."

"Maybe stolen?" Louie said. He grabbed the last piece of pizza, held it up over his head, tilted back and snapped up the bottom half.

I watched him chew.

"You talk to the police yet?"

"No, I think they had me medicated pretty fast last night. Heidi, acting as Nurse Ratched this morning, probably sprung me loose before they had a chance to interview me. I'm guessing they'll want to talk. They'll most likely phone, but that could be days from now. Not that I could tell them anything. Well, unless Manning gets hold of this, in which case I'll probably be charged with jaywalking, obstructing traffic, or even reckless driving if he could find a way to do that."

"Remember the other night? When you locked your keys in the car?"

"God, how could I forget? Damn near died of exposure walking home."

"You said you thought someone was following you. Maybe it was the same guy last night?"

"Yeah, maybe. But if it was, he had an entirely different car. That car I thought was following me was some sort of nondescript thing, silver or gray. I got a halfway decent look at it. This maniac last night, like I said I didn't get a good look, but I know for a fact it was some dark color.

172

Chapter Thirty-Nine

Heidi was back just before six. She dropped her red suitcase by the front stairs and carried a grocery bag out to the kitchen.

I slowly got off the couch and followed her.

She pulled a white plastic bag out of the brown paper grocery bag. The plastic bag held five little white carryout food containers. She arranged the containers, one next to the other according to height then using the edge of her hands pushed them into a straight line. "There, dinner is served. Get some plates and silverware out," she said then reached back into the grocery bag and pulled out a bottle of Prosecco.

"Prosecco?"

"Don't go there, Dev," she said and handed me the bottle. "Besides, you shouldn't even be drinking. Here, open this for me while I get a glass."

"You know I don't like this stuff."

"Amazingly, I didn't really have you in mind when I picked it up. Well, other than it might help me get through an evening of babysitting over here."

"You know what it does to you. Every time you drink this stuff you…"

"You're supposed to rest up and take it easy, anyway, cranky. Doctor's orders. And since you've got the energy to complain, once you've got my Prosecco opened you could take my suitcase upstairs. The guestroom," she instructed.

I looked up from the Prosecco cork. "I thought I was supposed to take it easy. Now I'm hauling stuff up a flight of stairs?"

"Don't even start," she said and pulled a champagne flute down from the cupboard.

After dinner, we settled in for a quiet evening with me reading on the couch while Heidi watched *Clueless* for the fifth or sixth time.

"Just don't wreck this movie with any of your jerky comments. Okay?"

I looked up from my book and smiled.

"Just don't, Dev," she said, then reached for the bottle and topped off her champagne flute with more Prosecco.

I bit my tongue and wondered how such an intelligent individual could ever be entertained by such drivel. There wasn't even a car chase scene. When the movie finally finished Heidi had both her legs curled up beneath her with her arms wrapped around one of the pillows from the couch.

"You want a drink? I need a Jameson."

"The hospital said you're not supposed to have any alcohol."

"I'm having a Jameson. Do you want anything?"

"I might have a little martini if you have any vodka."

I stopped at one Jameson. We chatted for maybe a half hour before we went upstairs. Heidi was leaning against the door frame as I got undressed. I heard her catch her breath when I took my shirt off. I gave an obvious wince as I pulled my T-shirt over my head.

"Oh Dev, honey, you're all banged up. You look like you were in a bomb…" she caught herself.

"Yeah, leave it to me to find the only IED in St. Paul."

It was supposed to be funny, along with my earlier complaints. I was making a play for her to climb in bed with me, but all of a sudden I snapped. "Someone tried to kill me, Heidi. They tried to kill me. I don't know who. I don't know why. What if the other guys had been there?"

I knew where this was going. I'd be hearing helicopters in about fifteen seconds, having a flashback and crawling under the bed if I didn't snap out of it. Suddenly, there she was with her arms around me, telling me not to worry and that I didn't do anything wrong and everything was okay. Everyone was safe, we all made it.

She held me and kept telling me, "Everyone is safe, Dev. It's okay. They're all okay."

She still had her arms around me when her snoring woke me up. We were under my duvet. Heidi was naked and I still had my jeans on. I laid there for a few minutes, mentally shaking my head for being such a big baby. I quietly climbed out of bed. I caught my reflection in the mirror and I had to admit I looked pretty bad, more black and blue than not. I gingerly pulled on a shirt and sweater, then glanced back at Heidi.

Somehow in the past ninety seconds she had angled herself across the bed, completely stretched out and was still snoring with a Prosecco accent. But she'd pulled me back from the brink last night. Stopped me from flipping out. Nurse Ratched? I don't think so, more like the sexiest guardian angel ever.

I was on my second cup of coffee when she came downstairs. She'd pulled one of my hockey jerseys on and was barefoot. She stared when she saw the plate piled high with caramel rolls.

"You go out and get those?"

"No, I baked them. Yeah, not to worry, I hit the bakery up the street."

"God, I shouldn't," she said as she pulled a roll off the pile and onto a small plate I'd set out. Strands of caramel fell across the granite counter top. "Any coffee left?" she asked as she bit into the caramel roll.

I poured a mug and slid it across the counter toward her.

"What?" she said, and stuffed a large bit of caramel and a small piece of roll into her mouth.

"You know what, thanks for being there for me last night."

"Yeah, can't tell you the last time someone kept their pants on when they climbed into bed with me." She laughed.

"You know what I mean."

She reached out and squeezed my hand. "You better get that checked out, Dev. That wasn't the first time."

I nodded, but didn't say anything.

"I'm serious. Have the VA…"

"How's that caramel roll?"

She gave me a little smile, but her eyes looked sad and had watered just a bit.

"They can help, you don't…" The she stopped herself, blinked and said. "It's delicious, I could eat the whole plate."

"I might just hold you to that."

"God, believe me I could do it."

Chapter Forty

I'd carried Heidi's suitcase out to her car and then watched from the sidewalk as she backed out of my driveway. She lowered her window as she pulled alongside of me.

"Thanks, Heidi. I really mean it, thank you for being here for me."

"I really meant what I said, Dev. Get it checked out." She stared at me for a long moment before she backed into the street, then gave a little wave and drove off.

Louie phoned about a half hour later.

"How we doing?"

"Just peachy. Now all I have to do is figure out what in the hell is going on."

"You coming in today?"

"I don't know, maybe see how I'm doing after lunch." Besides, I wanted to see if there was a movie on Netflix that wasn't a total waste of my time."

"You hear anything from the cops yet?"

"About the hit and run?"

"No, their daily updates on all the other cases they're investigating. Yes, the hit and run."

"Not a peep."

"Well, I'd guess they're probably just trying to sort out the paperwork before they get hold of you."

"Manning knows how to get hold of me."

"This probably hasn't even come onto his radar screen yet. When it does, you can bet you'll have that guy's undivided attention."

"Gee, I can hardly wait. You're not thinking I should get in touch with him again, are you?"

"As a matter of fact, since it worked so well for you the last time, no. The thought of talking with that guy hadn't even crossed my mind."

"I'd still like to know what the other night was all about."

"Well, you touched a nerve somewhere, and I'd say it's a pretty safe bet it's got nothing to do with job applications for that insurance company. That would seem to narrow the field down to your former client, Princess Danielle or super-jerk, Renee Paris if he's even alive."

I wasted another portion of my life clicking through a sub-par selection of B grade *free* movies on Netflix. Then I taxied down to the office after eating the two remaining caramel rolls for lunch.

I ran into Louie on the sidewalk outside. The subzero temperature had him walking like there was actually a purpose in life. He had climbed back into his wrinkled gray suit. He was carrying a newspaper and not wearing a coat. I guessed he was just heading back from a liquid lunch at The Spot.

"Well, the things you see when you don't have a gun," Louie said.

"Don't even joke. Anything shaking over at The Spot?"

"Usual. How you feeling?"

179

"A little tender around the edges, but I'll live." I glanced over to where the bus bench used to be. The metro transit folks had already been out and cleaned up the debris. If you weren't familiar with the corner you'd never know the thing was missing. There were still bits of my windshield and head lights glimmering along the curb near the intersection.

I sort of shook my head to get rid of any thoughts about the car incident, then held the door open for Louie as he scooted in, muttering his usual, "God, I hate this shit."

I was three steps behind him as he waddled up the stairs. I couldn't see around him and I felt the vibrations in my feet as he thundered up one step after another.

I glanced at the headlines in the paper when Louie tossed it across the picnic table. Not what you'd call a big news day. The Timberwolves lost again and some poor guy's car caught fire in a mall parking lot. We didn't have time to take our coats off before my phone rang.

"Haskell Investigations," I answered. A second later I heard the gum snap on the other end of the line. My heart sank as a voice growled my name.

"Haskell."

"Speaking," I said in a soft voice, knowing that might get to him.

"Haskell. This is Detective Norris Manning."

"Yes." I replied, sounding like I was anticipating some positive news. I think it gave him pause for a second, but only a second. Louie was giving me a questionable look. I made a scary face back at him, popped my eyes out and bared my teeth.

"Manning?" he whispered.

I nodded.

"I'd like you to grace us with your presence. Today if possible."

"I'd like to contact my legal representation, if I may. Would sometime tomorrow be acceptable? I've a pretty full afternoon scheduled."

"I'd prefer to see you today."

"I want to have counsel present. I'll have to get in touch with him and let you know."

"I could send a squad."

"You could."

There was another pause and I could hear Manning breathing on the other end. I was ready to joke about an obscene phone call when he said, "Get in touch with me the moment you hear from Laufen." Then he hung up.

"So?"

"You pretty much heard it. He wants to see me. I scammed some time for us, however long it's going to take me to contact you."

"I'm guessing that hit and run just popped up on Manning's radar screen."

"He didn't sound all that happy."

"How could you tell?" Louie chuckled.

Chapter Forty-One

"**This is Detective Norris** Manning. I'm located in interview room two, at approximately nine-o-seven AM. I'm joined by Mr. Devlin Haskell and his counsel, Mr. Louis Laufen. Gentlemen, could I have you state your names for the record, please?"

"Louie Laufen."

"Dev, Devlin Haskell."

"Thank you for joining me this morning. I'd like to start…"

"Excuse me, Detective, I'd like to start, if I may." I placed my briefcase on top of the Formica table and snapped open the locks. I reached in and grabbed what I was after, then watched the stunned look spread across Manning's face. The officer at the door had pushed himself off the wall and was watching me, nervously. Both his hands were resting on his webbed belt.

"I picked up these cinnamon rolls at a little bakery just up the street, Bon Vie. Are you familiar with it?" I smiled and drew a plastic wrapped paper plate with four frosted cinnamon rolls out of my briefcase. Manning's face grew a shade redder. The officer near the door visibly relaxed. Louie had a look of horror on his face that softened once he focused on the pastry.

182

"Come on, I got enough for all of us," I called over to the uniformed officer, relaxed again and leaning against the wall.

He gave a cautious glance at the back of Manning's shiny red head. "Thanks, but no thanks." He smiled.

"Perhaps later," Manning replied.

"Doughnuts more your thing?"

Manning took a deep breath and slowly exhaled. It struck me as possibly a calming routine he might have picked up from an anger management session. He pushed a manila envelope off to the side and opened the file in front of him. The typed form on the top of the file was upside down, so I couldn't read it.

"They're really good," I said and Louie slapped me on the thigh under the table.

"I know you're both busy. Let's get down to business, shall we?" Manning said, back in control.

"By all means," I said and smiled.

Manning took a long moment to pause and stare, reminding me this was his interview.

"What would you like from us, Detective?" Louie said, trying to calm the waters.

"Mr. Haskell, if you could account for your whereabouts over the past few days. What have you been up to?"

"Work mostly."

"In your office?"

"Sometimes. Up until three days ago I was in the office pretty much most of the day. Let's see, I got down there about ten, skipped lunch. I made a call on someone around two, back behind my desk right after that. I was gone I'd say probably no more than an hour. I had a planning meeting with Mr. Laufen early that evening, then on my way home I was involved in a hit

183

and run accident. I woke up in the hospital the following morning. I was discharged that afternoon…"

"Back up for a moment and let's start at the beginning. Tell me more about your call that afternoon. You visited a client?"

'Here we go.' I thought. "Actually, no. It was a business call, personal business."

"To see?"

"An attorney by the name of Richard Hedstrom."

"And you went to his office?"

"No, sir, his residence."

"Not his office?"

"Actually, I didn't know where his office was to be honest. I still don't know. I took a chance he might be at home and hoped he'd have time to see me. Unfortunately, it's a gated community and I couldn't get past the security guard."

Manning nodded like the security guard not allowing me in seemed the natural thing for anyone to do. He waited another long moment. "And then?"

"And then I went back to my office. Mr. Laufen and I had a planning meeting early that evening and I was on my way home when I was involved in an accident."

Manning nodded and looked hopeful at the mention of my accident, like it just might have been the most positive occurrence of my day. Then he said, "I'm not quite following. The security guard wouldn't admit you?"

"That's right. He tried to reach Mr. Hedstrom by phone, but couldn't and so he told me I'd have to come back later. I get it. I mean, after all it is a secure area, theoretically."

"So you just left?"

"Yep. The guard had been kind enough to provide me with Mr. Hedstrom's phone number. I attempted to phone him, but I got a recorded message. Something about his message center being full, if I recall."

"You went to his residence without an appointment?"

"Yeah, I just hoped to get lucky. And obviously, I didn't."

That seemed to please Manning and he nodded again.

"How well did you know Mr. Hedstrom?"

"To the best of my knowledge, not at all. I can't recall ever meeting him."

Manning nodded like this made perfect sense. "So to the best of your knowledge you never met him?"

"Like I just said, not that I can recall."

Manning jotted a quick note.

"You were never in his office?"

"Not that I can recall. To the best of my knowledge, I have no idea where it's even located."

Manning made a check mark and jotted a couple of words after that.

"And you've never been in his condominium?"

"If you mean the one in the Viagra Triangle, no, I've only been as far as the guard station." I smiled and shot a glance at Louie who remained straight faced.

"By Viagra Triangle, you're referring to the River View Terrace development?"

"Yeah, that's right, River View Terrace."

"And you've never been in Mr. Hedstrom's condominium, nor his office, nor to the best of your recollection ever met the man. Is that correct?"

I thought that pretty much wrapped things up nice and tight. "Yeah, that's correct."

"Have you ever gained access to the River View Terrace complex, Mr. Haskell?"

"Yes, once. I think it was six or maybe even seven years ago. I attended an anniversary celebration for Mr. and Mrs. Martin Dempsey. I accompanied their daughter, Monica."

"And that's the only time you were allowed access to the complex."

"Yes, the anniversary celebration was actually in the Dempsey condominium. I haven't been back since. I believe Martin Dempsey passed away a few years ago. I don't know if his wife still lives there."

Manning flipped some pages in the file, and ran his finger down a list of some sort. "According to our records I see a Ms. Monica Dempsey filed a restraining order against you. Same individual?"

"Well, she dumped me the next morning, after the party. It was sort of a misunderstanding between the two of us and a former acquaintance of mine. A sort of dancer woman we ran into later that night."

Louie shot me a quick glance.

"A dancer, one can only imagine," Manning said. He nodded, but didn't make a note. Instead, he reached for the manila envelope lying next to his file. He gently held the thing and carefully reached his hand inside treating whatever was in the envelope like it contained all of his future hopes and dreams. He began to pull his hand out of the envelope, but stopped midway. The envelope had some sort of bar code sticker affixed to the upper left hand corner and below that a six digit number written in black marker. I caught the hint of a plastic bag grasped in Manning's hand.

"Mr. Haskell, I'm wondering if you would be able to help us identify this item. Let the record show this is evidence file number one-three-two-zero-zero-nine,"

Manning said, reading the number off the envelope. Then he pulled the plastic evidence bag from the manila envelope. There was a black leather belt rolled up inside the evidence bag. The belt had a silver buckle sporting a Celtic design.

Manning didn't have to remove the belt from the plastic bag. The moment I saw it I already knew the belt had a silver buckle as well as a tab with a Celtic knot design. The black leather was an inch and a half wide and expertly hand tooled, with a fairly involved Celtic border design that butted either side of script letters spelling out *Devlin Haskell,* my name, across the back of the belt.

My pal Bobby had made the belt for me maybe two years ago. My mind wandered back to the last time I'd seen the thing. Danielle was wearing it along with a contented smile. We'd been playing bucking bronco, her idea, and I had been hanging on for all I was worth.

"Mr. Haskell?"

"Oh, yeah, I was just thinking. Well, that would appear to be a belt like one I had."

"Do you think it might be the same belt?"

"Possibly."

"I wonder if we might examine that a little closer, Detective," Louie asked and extended his hand across the table.

"By all means, please, be my guest."

"Dev?" Louie placed the plastic bag in front of me and looked at me hopefully.

There was a slim, half-percent chance there might be two belts like this in the world. Two guys in town with a belt that had my name tooled across the back of it. That chance quickly disappeared when I saw my phone number written on the inside of the belt just next to the buckle. *"So when you leave it in the backseat of*

187

some woman's car she can still call you and give it back," Bobby had joked. Only right now it wasn't sounding quite as funny, sitting here in Interview Room Two.

"Does this belt look in any way familiar, Mr. Haskell?" Manning looked extremely pleased with himself, enjoying the moment.

"Yes, this is my belt. It's been missing for a week, maybe two."

"Really?" Manning smiled.

"Yeah, I've been looking for it."

"Do you think it was stolen? Are you suggesting someone may have gained access to your home and stole this belt?"

"Well…"

"Did you report the break in?"

"Well…"

"You see Mr. Haskell, this belt was found in Mr. Hedstrom's condominium. Under his bed, I believe our investigation indicates." He smiled coldly, and then slid an evidence form across the table to me. Attached to the form was a photo of my belt lying under a bed. It was my turn to hit Louie on the thigh and I did, repeatedly.

"I wonder if I might have a private moment to discuss with my client," Louie said.

"Certainly, five minutes enough time?" Manning asked just a little too sweetly for my taste.

188

Chapter Forty-Two

"**Dev?**" **Louie stared at** me wide eyed. What the…"

"I know what you're going to say, Louie."

"Really?"

"Well…"

"Shut up and listen. How'd your belt get in Dick Head's place? Were you ever actually in there?"

"No. Honest. I never met the guy. I've never been in his condo, ever."

"Well, how in the hell did your belt end up under his damn bed?" Louie was red faced and almost shaking he was so mad.

"I don't know. I mean it, Louie. I have absolutely no idea. The last time I saw that belt it was wrapped around Danielle's waist."

"God damn it, Dev." He nodded toward my lap. "You ought to cut that damn thing off with all the trouble it gets you into."

My eyes grew wide as I stared at him.

"I'm not kidding, when are you going to stop thinking with the wrong head? Damn it. Okay, let's think here. I'd say it's a pretty safe bet at this stage that Danielle is tied up with Dick Head somehow."

"I guess so."

"You think? Jesus Christ. Okay, first thing, her client privilege just went out the damn window. You're giving her name to Manning."

The door suddenly creaked open and Manning poked his bald head in. It had the look of a shiny globe, the ceiling light over the door reflected off his smooth, pink skin. "All set, gentlemen?"

"Another minute or two," Louie half shouted over his shoulder.

"We'll be out here in the hall, just knock on the door whenever you're ready," Manning said, sounding just a little too chipper for my taste. Then he pulled the door closed.

"Prick," I said under my breath.

"I have a sick feeling he's just getting warmed up," Louie said. "Dev, you've been compromised here. I want you to give Manning any and all of your Danielle Roxbury information. At this stage, you're not just aiding their investigation, you're protecting yourself. Does the term 'set-up' have any connotations? Sorry to say, but I think this woman has been playing you like a fiddle. Your belt under Dick Head's bed Jesus Christ."

"I think…"

"Save it," Louie said, then stood up, walked over and knocked on the door. "Ready whenever you are, Detective."

Manning strolled in carrying his thick file in one hand and the manila evidence envelope with my belt in the other. He was looking fresh and happy. The uniformed officer stepped in behind him, closed the door and leaned back against the wall. The interview room suddenly seemed to smell of desperation.

"So, you were just about to tell me how your belt ended up beneath a bed in a condominium you've never been inside of." Manning sat back, folded his arms and smiled contentedly. His eyes bored into me.

"Yeah, well, the only explanation I have is that I left that belt, my belt, at the home of my client. Her name is Danielle Roxbury. She's the client we discussed the other day. The client I was representing when I met with Renee Paris and discussed his outstanding loan."

"Really." Manning nodded, but didn't make any notes. It was almost as if he knew all this. He smiled again and looked comfortable with his arms contentedly folded across his chest.

I thought, *'Oh, shit.'*

"Oh, yes, that's right, your so called *discussion* with Mr. Paris. That was the assault we viewed on the security tape, wasn't it? At Casey's? Just prior to the big fire there?"

I nodded.

"I'm sorry, Mr. Haskell, would you speak up, please?

"Yes."

"So, you were representing Danielle Roxbury at the time of that little incident?"

"Yes."

"And she informed you that Mr. Paris was in debt to her for, I believe you stated in an earlier interview, a sum of fifty thousand dollars. Does that sound about right?"

"Yes, that's the amount she told me."

"A lot of money, fifty grand," Manning said.

I nodded, and then absently said, "Yeah, all in cash."

Louie's head shot up with a very surprised look.

191

"Cash? Really? Did she happen to mention when this transaction occurred? When she gave Mr. Paris fifty-thousand-dollars in cash?"

"Not specifically, no. I, I guess she didn't. She just sort of said sometime in the last year, I'm not sure. I never actually got an exact date."

"What sort of documentation did she show you? A signed note? A letter of intent? Perhaps a securities pledge?"

"No, nothing like that."

"Really? Well, then, what documentation *did* she show you?"

"Actually, I sort of just took her at her word. She told me she had lent him the money and that Mr. Paris had promised to pay her back. Then she mentioned that she'd been unable to contact him and she felt he was avoiding her. She gave me a phone number to call along with his address."

"Fifty thousand dollars. In cash. Wow, and she basically just handed it over. Does that strike you as strange, Mr. Haskell?"

"Well, yeah now that you mention it. I mean, I thought it was kind of different, you know when she told me."

"Kind of different. She just gave the man fifty grand. Handed it over to him and then apparently just walked away without a care in the world."

"I suppose in retrospect, yeah it does sound a little strange."

Manning nodded like I was finally making sense. "But you trusted her?"

"Yes."

"And even though she said she's been unable to contact Mr. Paris, she just happened to have his address and phone number. And she passed them on to you?"

"Yeah."

"Did you knock on Mr. Paris's door?"

"No, I drove past his house, but it was vacant. It had been posted unfit by the city. I think it's a category three building."

Manning nodded. "And his phone?"

"That's how I set up the appointment to meet him, I called the phone number."

"The same number Danielle Roxbury gave you when she said she was unable to contact Mr. Paris? That phone number?"

"No, not exactly."

"Oh?"

"See, the number she gave me didn't work. So, I tracked him down through his business number. The one for his Bar-B-Que sauces, LuSifer's. I got it from a grocery chain."

"I see, and you spoke with him when you called?"

"No, I left a message, he returned my call that evening and we set up a meeting for the following afternoon."

"How many times did you have to call him?"

"Just once."

"Funny your client, Ms. Roxbury, had been unable to reach him."

"I don't know."

"So, we saw the tape of your *meeting* with Mr. Paris. And then what? You gave Ms. Roxbury that personalized belt as a symbol of your trust and continued support?"

"Not exactly. I believe I just left that behind. I must have forgotten it at her home I guess. I sort of made a mental note to pick it up the next time we got together."

Manning nodded again which made me even more worried.

"Fair to say you were in a sexual relationship with Ms. Roxbury?"

"Mmm-mmm, I wouldn't go that far."

"You did have sex with her, correct?"

"Yes."

"And just for the sake of argument, if you left your belt at her home, this wasn't some fifteen second spur of the moment, wham-bam, flash in the pan now, was it?"

"Well, no, not exactly."

"After all, Mr. Haskell, you've got a bit of a reputation. Fair to say Ms. Roxbury no doubt enjoyed herself?"

"Yes." I nodded and smiled at the memory.

"Was that her form of payment to you? The sex."

"What? Oh, no, Danielle, Ms. Roxbury paid me in cash. Ten hundred dollar bills, a thousand dollars."

"In cash you say?"

"Yes. She delivered them herself."

"Wow, cash seems to be how she likes to operate. Does that happen often in your line of work? Gosh, I can't remember the last time I saw a grand in cash."

"It happens once in a while. It's not completely unusual."

Manning looked down, flipped some pages in his file, and read for a moment while Louie and I exchanged glances. Manning looked back up at me with a puzzled expression on his face.

"See, our question is where would she have gotten a thousand dollars in cash? Or for that matter the fifty thousand you say she gave Mr. Paris?"

"I suppose she stopped at her bank and made a withdrawal."

"Yeah, you'd think that, but her accounts have been closed for some time. As a matter of fact, her bank has initiated legal proceedings against her."

"I think she has a trust fund, and well, she owns that big mansion."

"Funny you should mention that. Actually, we've been looking, pretty thoroughly I might add, and we found no evidence of a trust fund, anywhere. I'm not suggesting one might not exist, but if it does we've been unable to find any record of it. Actually, the only bank accounts we found for Ms. Roxbury were closed by the bank over a year ago. She apparently took out an equity loan on her home back in 2006. She's been in arrears on that property for over two years and the bank has begun foreclosure proceedings. Seems she's also in arrears on her property taxes and Ramsey County has begun proceedings as well."

"I, I had no idea."

"And yet somehow, you tell me she managed to give fifty thousand dollars, cash, to Renee Paris and one thousand dollars in cash, to you. How do you think she was able to pull that off?"

"I, I don't know," I said. I was in shock.

"Now, we have Richard Hedstrom," Manning said, switching gears. "I have to tell you, Mr. Haskell. I'm a little confused. Our investigation indicates that he was in a partnership with Mr. Paris, a number of partnerships, actually. You assaulted Mr. Paris. An item of yours, this belt, was found in Mr. Hedstrom's residence." Manning nodded at the evidence envelope. "The same residence you recently attempted to gain access to. Now, we learn that Mr. Hedstrom was reported missing as of three days ago."

"I don't know anything about that. This is the first I've heard of it."

"Are you at all familiar with a dark blue 2013 Audi A6?"

I had no idea where Manning was going with this. I shook my head blankly and muttered, "No."

"It is, or rather was, Mr. Hedstrom's vehicle. Apparently, someone took it for a joyride, smashed it up, removed the plates and then set it ablaze in a shopping mall parking lot the other night. Now, we can't seem to locate Richard Hedstrom, Renee Paris or Danielle Roxbury."

"You've been looking for her, Danielle?"

"Yes." Manning nodded, and flipped some more pages in his file. "Apparently, we're not the only ones. We have a record of a number of calls made to Ms. Roxbury from this cell phone number at various times of the day and night." Manning took a page from his file and passed it across the table to me. "Interestingly, by checking the various cell towers we can be about ninety nine point nine percent sure that a number of these calls were made by someone actually located in Ms. Roxbury's home. Would you happen to recognize this cell phone number?"

I didn't really have to look, but I did, anyway.

"That's my cell phone number. Actually, I wasn't in her house. I was parked out in front on the street. I think one time I may have even been on her front porch."

"Out in front of her home or on her front porch? Interesting. It's been below zero for the past month. Why not just ring her doorbell?"

"I did, but she wasn't home. At least, she didn't answer when I rang."

"Amazing she wouldn't let *you* in. Maybe she thought you were coming back for another payment? Back for more sex? Maybe she was just in the shower,

196

you know, getting spruced up for you. Can't say that I really blame you. After all, she's a very attractive woman, isn't she, Haskell?"

"No. I mean, no, I wasn't coming back for more sex. I just wanted to check on her. Make sure Paris hadn't been stalking her or attacked her or something."

"Gee, that's very noble of you. And, what about that car belonging to Richard Hedstrom? Set ablaze in the middle of the night in a shopping mall parking lot. You wouldn't have just happened to pass by at about that time, would you, Mr. Haskell? Maybe you wanted to ask him about your belt?"

"Actually." I smiled back at Manning. "I saw the headline on that and I was sedated in the hospital that night until sometime after noon the following day. I have a witness who can attest to the fact I was home the entire evening until ten the following morning when she departed. At that point I had to taxi to my office and I'm sure somewhere the taxi service would have a record of that."

"Was it Danielle Roxbury *caring* for you until ten the following morning? We've been trying to reach her." Manning sneered across the table at me.

"No, the woman's name is Heidi Bauer. She's a long time friend and she merely wanted to make sure I was all right after having been involved in that accident and released from the hospital earlier in the day."

"Does Danielle Roxbury know?" Manning shot back.

"Actually, I did receive a phone call from her. But not from the phone number she had given me earlier."

Manning looked genuinely surprised.

"I have it on my cell. Here just a minute," I said and dug my cell out.

"So you've heard from her recently, the Roxbury woman?" Manning asked, recovering.

"Yes, here's the number. Louie, I mean Mr. Laufen was with me when her call came through, we were in our office at the time."

"I can attest to that, Detective," Louie said.

Manning seemed to deflate slightly when Louie backed me up. He made a note of Danielle's new phone number in his file. Then he paged through a number of reports in the file, but didn't ask any questions. Eventually, he looked up at us.

"I guess that will do for right now. I'd like you to stay in touch, Mr. Haskell. You're not under arrest, at this time. But I think it would be wise if you're planning any travel you might just contact our office first.

Louie and I nodded together.

Manning gave a long sigh, like he'd been so close, yet had somehow missed. "I guess unless you gentlemen have any questions that will conclude our interview, for the time being anyway."

We both shook our heads and Manning had the uniformed officer escort us down to the elevators. Once the doors closed behind us we signaled one another to keep quiet.

Chapter Forty-Three

"No, please don't say a thing. Just give me a moment to think here," Louie said as we bounced across pot holes on our way out of the parking lot.

"That was Hedstrom's car someone torched the other night?" I said.

Louie sighed, then said, "Well, smashed up first and then torched once they pulled the plates off. Bit of a coincidence I'd say, just after someone tried to run you down. You sure you didn't get a look at that car? An Audi A6 sleek, fast and dark blue?"

"I can attest to the sleek, fast and dark bit, but that's about it. I can't ID the vehicle, it all happened too fast. What the hell, Danielle's broke?"

Louie looked over at me for a long moment, then said, "She's more than just broke. Broke suggests a zero balance. It sounds like right now your little lady friend is running heavily into the negative numbers."

"But I don't get it. That huge damn house of hers?"

"Pledged at the peak of the boom and then lost, apparently. She wouldn't be the first person that happened to."

"But, Louie, her trust fund?"

"I'm guessing the generations before her pissed most of it away and she probably still can't believe she went through whatever was left. God forbid she'd ever have to work like the rest of us."

"Richard Hedstrom?"

"Dick Head? Obviously he's tied in somewhere, Manning as much as said the guy's invested in a number of different partnerships with Paris. Maybe he did the same thing for this Danielle that you did?"

I looked at Louie and he shook his head.

"No, not that," he said. "Maybe she just followed your advice and hired some legal attack dog. Dick Head just delivered the same message to Paris that you did. Only he was a bit more understated and I'm guessing no one has it on tape."

"And then what? She straps on my belt and goes over to Hedstrom's place to play ride 'em cowboy?"

"I don't know, maybe. To be honest, that really isn't anywhere near your biggest problem right now."

"It just doesn't sound like the woman I know."

"The woman you know? Dev. Hello. Did you hear what Manning said in there? The woman you know doesn't exist. Apparently, she never did. She has no funds, she owes back taxes and she's in the process of losing her big old inherited house. We don't really know for sure if she even gave Paris the fifty grand, let alone in cash. And in her spare time it looks like she could well be rolling around with Dick Head."

"Yeah, but I mean other than that."

Louie looked over at me.

"Relax, I'm kidding," I said.

"Oh, well, good thing you can find something to laugh about. Just remember, Manning would still like to hang that fire at Casey's and I'm presuming Renee Paris or whoever got roasted in there, around your neck.

Don't think for a minute he's given up, he's just gathering more ammunition, Dev."

"Yeah. Where do you think they are? Danielle and Paris and Hedstrom?"

"God, who in the hell knows? They could all be together sitting on a beach somewhere for all the good it would do us. I doubt it, but stranger things have happened. We know someone ended up in that fire it might be one of them, Paris has my vote. We know Danielle is still out there, somewhere. And Dick Head Hedstrom, good Lord, who knows?"

"Think they're still in town?"

"I wouldn't be," Louie said and then pulled to the curb in front of our office.

We got out and Louie walked around the car. We stood on the sidewalk and he looked from the door leading up to our second story office, then over to The Spot. "You thinking what I'm thinking?"

"Couldn't make things any worse," I said.

"Okay, but just one," Louie said and we crossed the street.

Chapter Forty-Four

Louie bought a round, then I bought a round, just the one round each.

"Discipline," Louie cautioned and we headed back out the door.

"I don't know where to begin," I said once we were up in the office.

"Well, about the only advice I can give you is to stay the hell out of Manning's way," Louie said and tossed his coat on the picnic table.

I stared out the window for the better part of the next hour. Then, since I didn't want Manning wise to my efforts, I wasted my time attempting to call Danielle from a pay phone around the corner. Not so amazingly, no one answered. I almost froze to death in the process.

I borrowed Louie's car and drove past Paris' house which, at no surprise, turned out to be a complete waste of my time. The only difference from the last time I'd seen the place was that the snow had drifted deeper across the sidewalk.

My drive past Danielle's home was much the same. The place looked occupied with the walks shoveled and snow melting on the roof indicating the heat was on. But at four-thirty on a December afternoon there were no lights on inside and I didn't catch as much as a twitch from a curtain or window shade. I didn't call her from my cell for fear Manning would be alerted. I got out and rang her doorbell, another waste of my time. I should have just stayed in Louie's car where it was warm.

On the drive back to the office I was thinking about Hedstrom's condo. If he was there, with the guard's denying access to everyone at the front gate it could serve as the perfect safe haven for Danielle. At least up until Manning burst through the door and started looking under the beds, again. I was still thinking of the condo two hours later, sitting next to Louie at The Spot.

"One more and that's it for me, Linda," he said, then pushed his glass across the bar and turned on his stool to face me.

"You got time to drop me off so I can do some cross country skiing tonight?" I asked.

"Are you crazy? It's fifteen below out there and dropping. That's not counting the damn wind chill."

"I need to get rid of some stress, not to mention burn some of these calories off before I start developing a pair of love handles," I said, then took a sip of my Mankato Ale, not adding the *'and ending up like you'* part of that statement.

"Yeah, I suppose. God knows I haven't been able to stop you from doing all the other incredibly stupid things up to this point. I guess there's absolutely no reason I'd think I could stop you now."

"Thanks, I just need to change and grab my stuff. You can drop me off along the river. I'll hop on one of the trails down there."

"How are you going to get home?"

"Not to worry, I'll figure something out."

203

He stared at me warily over the rim of his fresh drink, drained most of it and then said, "As you're legal counsel I do not want to know."

"Relax, I'm just…"

"No," he said and thrust the palm of his hand out toward me. "Stop, not another word. Come on, let's get it over with. Then I'm going somewhere with plenty of folks around who'll be able to attest to the fact I was nowhere near you tonight."

Chapter Forty-Five

Louie dropped me off about a half mile from the Viagra Triangle. We hadn't exchanged so much as a word on the drive down to the river.

"See if you can pull off up here, there's a sort of parking lot thing for tourists and stuff to look at the river," I directed.

Louie pulled into the viewing area. Amazingly it had been plowed. I could actually see the lights from the upper floors of the condo buildings as I took my skis out from the back of his car. I stepped into them, snapped the bindings into the low cut boots then slid around to the driver's side. Louie lowered his window a bit.

"Be careful and stay warm," he said then sped off before I could say anything.

Another car pulled in as Louie left. The thing was sort of a non-descript gray and between the night sky and the tinted windows it was too dark to see into the vehicle. I guessed it was probably just a couple of teenagers looking for a private place to explore the differences between one another.

Three minutes later I was skiing across what looked like a picnic area for the River View Terrace

205

condominiums. You could just make out the tops of the picnic tables buried beneath almost three feet of snow.

In a way, coming in by this route wasn't that surprising. All the pomp and circumstance of a guard shack with guys wearing military sweaters and embroidered badges. No doubt they had ranked titles like Sergeant and Captain. The fancy gate out front where people like me were denied access made everyone in the complex feel safe and warm. Meanwhile, I'd just waltzed into the area through a side entrance and on skis, no less.

There were five buildings making up the River View Terrace complex and Hedstrom's was number three, directly in the middle and positioned right on the bend in the river. From his fourth floor condo he'd have a gorgeous view in a number of different directions.

I skied right up to the front door of the building, stepped out of my skis and carried them inside. I was dressed for it, the skiing. I had on a heavy wool sweater, dark blue with large white snowflakes the size of a fifty-cent piece in the pattern, a matching knitted cap and mittens. The outfit had been a Valentine's Day gift from Kristen, a Minneapolis Swedish girl who later threatened to have her brothers throttle me if I ever revealed her penchant for chocolate sauce in bed. Her secret remained safe with me.

The building entrance was granite floored, with a dozen locked mail boxes set into a brick wall. Tall glass panels looked into the building's carpeted lobby complete with upholstered furniture, four matching end tables sporting lamps and an elevator. A phone on the wall next to the mail boxes allowed you to contact the individual units. Hedstrom, R was listed as unit number 402, so much for tight security.

I dialed the number and waited. Fortunately, no one answered. I was still listening to the phone ring when a couple came out of elevator and headed for the door of the lobby. I waited for them to open the security door then said, "Okay, Mom, I'll be right up."

I pegged them as maybe in their mid-to-late-sixties. She was blonde, in a floor length dark fur coat and matching turban hat. The guy had a neatly trimmed mustache and wore an expensive looking camel colored cashmere coat. He had placed a brown fedora on his head as they exited the elevator. I held the security door for them once she opened it and walked out. He paused and gave me a look that seemed a little unsure while he pulled on sleek, brown leather driving gloves.

"Lovely sweater, cold night for it," the woman said. She nodded at my outfit and smiled with a sort of far away look, maybe remembering similar distant nights.

"Yes ma'am," I replied.

The good manners seemed to alleviate any fears he had and she smiled back.

"Stay warm," I called after them, then ducked inside, stepped onto the elevator and pushed the button for the fourth floor.

The elevator opened onto a 'V' shaped hallway with beige carpeting, lighter beige walls and steel trim around the doors. Brushed aluminum wall sconces in sort of an art nouveau style illuminated the hall. A hint of some sort of classical music was coming from a distant unit off to the left. Number 402, Hedstrom's place was straight ahead.

I knocked softly and held my finger over the peephole, praying no one answered. I studied the two locks on the door, both manufactured by Schlage. It said so right on the locks.

I waited a good minute and a half. It only seemed like a year standing in the hall with my heart pounding in my ears. I took my pick set out and went to work. Not surprisingly I had both locks clicked open in a couple of minutes. As was the case with a number of high security complexes, the actual security was at the castle gate. Once you made it past that things became relatively easy.

I opened the door to the unit, stepped inside and hurriedly closed the door behind me. I was listening and at the same time checking frantically for any indication of an alarm system. I needn't have worried. It turned out Hedstrom didn't have one.

I held my place for a good five minutes with my ears strained. Other than my heartbeat I couldn't hear a thing. Even in the dark I began to get a sense of the unit's layout. It was spacious, with windows at a right angle on either side of a fireplace providing a fantastic view up and down river. Even tonight, at close to twenty below and with more snow beginning to swirl outside, it was gorgeous. The moon had risen above the horizon and although you couldn't really see it you had the sense of it glowing up there, just behind the clouds.

As my eyes adjusted the furnishings came into view, contemporary and comfortable. The focal point of the living room was a gas fireplace. The room itself sported a large oriental rug. Two couches, a couple of end tables with lamps and then, of course, the marvelous view of the river on either side of the fireplace. Off to the right was a chandeliered dining area with an elegant table seating eight and matching marble topped side cabinets. Behind the dining room there looked to be a fairly large kitchen area.

Off to the left, on the other side of the living room was a hallway with a series of closed doors, four to be exact. I headed cautiously down the hall, ears strained for the slightest noise. The first door was an office, complete with a fairly large desk, a computer, and a flat screen mounted on the wall. The desk was positioned in front of some built in closets.

The room next to the office was a guest room sporting a matching bedroom set consisting of a double bed, a dresser, a makeup table and mirror. There was a little sort of stool with a needle point cushion in front of the makeup table. More built in closets were along the far wall.

Across the hall was the master bedroom with an attached bathroom. A king sized, four poster bed dominated the room. A carved antique chest sat at the foot of the bed. The bed was high enough and positioned against the wall so you could lie in bed all day and just look at the river view out the window. Two large chests of drawers were lined up against the inside wall. The view out of the window was marvelous, looking out over the city's downtown and then past all the lights down river to the bluffs and another bend in the Mississippi. A door led to the attached bathroom.

I recognized the carpet and the base of the bed post from the evidence picture Manning had shown me of my belt. I checked under the bed, but nothing was there.

Gorgeous as it was, the condo was empty. I quietly began to search, not knowing what I was searching for. Based on the contents of the closets and the chests of drawers this was strictly a guy's place. Men's clothes, shoes, a twenty-gauge shotgun along with some duck calls, boots, two softball bats. There was some women's clothing, but not enough to suggest permanent residence. More like the casual visitor or a short stay. Perhaps Hedstrom had a girlfriend, or maybe he just had a daughter who came to visit.

There were two empty coffee cups in the kitchen sink, one with lipstick. It struck me as strange that if Manning's crew had been through here a few days back they would have left the coffee cups. Logic would seem to suggest they'd have taken the things and maybe finger printed them in a lab, or possibly here on site. Of course, maybe the cops just made some coffee, I had no idea.

I checked the dishwasher, it was empty. The refrigerator held nothing of note. Four cans of Lite beer, no thanks. The usual ketchups, mustard, salad dressing sort of things you'd find in any place. There was nothing that looked like a plate of leftovers from last night or a platter of steak to be cooked tomorrow. Then again, maybe Hedstrom was the sort who just ate out every night.

I went through the office area, but didn't find anything of note. The computer required a password and a security code so I couldn't gain access. What paper files there were yielded nothing out of the ordinary.

It was after eleven when I stopped poking around and wandered back into the living room. With the curtains pulled back, despite the late hour the room seemed to be lit from the outside. The view in both directions was beautiful. I sat down on the couch, stared out the window and waited.

Chapter Forty-Six

"Thinking maybe I'll fix myself a little drinky pooh, you want one?"

The voice in my dream didn't sound like me.

"I think you've had more than enough for one night," a woman replied.

That certainly sounded familiar, but the exchange seemed to be interrupting my otherwise deep sleep. A light flicked on somewhere and the next thing I knew someone half shouted, "What the hell are you doing here?" then hit me on the side of the head as I was yanked off the couch.

I rolled toward the fireplace a couple of times, aware there was a pair of feet after me. I was growing more awake by the second. A foot kicked out and missed me. I was on my knees when the second kick came. I caught it solidly in the midsection, held on to the shoe, twisted at the ankle and pushed back. I felt something crackle and give way in my grip just as the guy went down.

"Ahhh-hhhh, Jesus Christ," the figure cursed. He clawed at an end table for balance, dragging a table lamp down on top of him in the process.

"Stop it. Stop it or I swear I'll shoot you. I mean it, Dev."

I'd just gotten to my feet ready to kick back when I turned and looked at Danielle Roxbury. She was holding a small revolver in her demure little hand. Blued steel from the look of the thing with hatched wooden grips. I guessed it was a .38. She was pointing it at me with an outstretched arm and glaring eyes.

"Danielle?"

"I mean it, Dev, stop or so help me I'll shoot you. I swear to God, I will."

"I believe you, Danielle, could you maybe just point that thing somewhere else?"

"Ahhh-hhhh, my ankle, God, you maniac. I think you broke it," Renee Paris groaned on the floor in a quasi-fetal position, clutching his ankle.

"See if you can get up, Renee," Danielle said.

He wrestled with the table lamp on the floor for a moment before he tossed it off to the side. As the shade bounced off the floor I heard the bulb break.

"Renee, stop it, someone will hear you," Danielle said.

"God, my ankle, I don't know if I can walk," he said, then gingerly hobbled to his feet and attempted to walk back and forth. His limp was pronounced and he held on to the back of the couch for balance. "God damn it," he groaned with every step.

Danielle rolled her eyes. "I'm sure you'll live, Renee," she said, then fixed me with a wild stare and motioned toward the couch with the gun. "Sit down, Dev. What, exactly, are you doing here?"

"I could ask you two the same thing."

"No, you couldn't, not really, I've got the gun."

"God," Paris groaned and limped into the dining room.

"What are you doing here?"

"I wanted to check on Richard Hedstrom. The police showed me a photo of my belt. It was lying under the bed in there. Thanks for that, you remember my belt?"

"Most unfortunate. They missed us by no more than a minute or two, thank God. Apparently, his sister is worried and contacted them. Of course, Renee burning the car did nothing to help." She'd raised her voice slightly as she looked over toward the dining room.

"I almost had you, you bastard," Paris said, then limped out of the kitchen with a glass of something that looked pretty strong.

"Renee, no. You've had enough."

"I can…" He stopped whatever he was going to say and slammed the glass down on the end table. Some of the liquid splashed out of the glass and onto the table top. Even in the half light I could make out reddish marks on the side of his face where his skin had blistered after our last conversation.

"We're going to have to deal with this before morning, Renee. You'll have to get the car and wait for us out front."

"I think we should…"

But a look from Danielle cut him off again. "I'm going to need your help here, Renee, and then the car. Why don't you just lie face down on the rug, Dev?"

"Too bad the cops took my belt, we could…"

"I don't care to hear about it, just get down there," she said and waved the pistol for added effect.

"Oh, God," Paris hissed and limped around in a sort of circle.

"Renee, that little drawer at the end of the kitchen counter, there's an extension cord in there, get it."

213

"I'm not sure I…"

"Just do it, Renee, for God's sake."

I heard him groan as he hobbled away and into the kitchen. It sounded like he pulled a drawer open, then groaned with every step as he limped back into the living room. "Will this do?"

"Perfect. Wrap his hands behind his back."

"I…"

"Renee, just once would you please…"

"All right, God, this hurts," he said as he made his way around the couch, then half collapsed on top of me, driving a knee into the back of my rib cage.

"Ahhh-hhhh," I groaned.

"Not so good, is it? Being on the receiving end."

I was gasping for breath as he pulled my arms back and wrapped the cord tightly around my wrist.

"Make sure he won't get loose," Danielle said.

"He won't, believe me, I've got it nice and tight," Paris said, then slowly got back on his feet. He attempted to kick me, but he half fell into the couch when the injured ankle gave way. His foot just glanced off my side. "Arghhh, God damn it."

"Renee, will you please stop? Get to your feet, Dev," Danielle said. I heard her voice fading slightly. She seemed to be moving down the hallway toward the bedroom.

"I'm not sure I can, you've got my hands tied up behind my damn…"

She was suddenly there, stomping up next to me. She pulled the hammer back on the revolver with an audible click, then pressed the barrel against the back of my head. Her voice had suddenly gone several octaves higher and she sounded like she was ready to snap. "I swear to God, I'm going to shoot the both of you if you

214

don't start cooperating. Do you hear me? Well?" she half shrieked.

"Yes," I said, familiar with women snapping and going off the deep end.

"Renee, do you hear me? I'm not kidding," she screamed and then pushed the gun barrel harder into the back of my head for added emphasis. I guess she was threatening Renee with having to clean up the mess if she blew my brains out.

"Okay, calm down, Danielle. What do you need?" Paris said.

"Help me get him up."

Renee hobbled over and the two of them pulled me to my feet, then half-walked, half-dragged me down the hallway toward the master bedroom. I could smell the alcohol coming off Paris as he hobbled along, bouncing back and forth between the wall and me, groaning with every other step.

"Wow, this is really kinky. Are you going to make him watch the two of us, Danielle? Or were you thinking a three-way, because…"

"Shut up, Dev," she said, then pulled me into the bathroom. She tore the shower curtain back and turned the water on.

"Get in there," she commanded.

I gave her a questioning look.

"Oh, God," she said, and placed her hand in the shower spray to check the temperature. She adjusted the control slightly. "There, now get in and stay put. Renee, help him in so he doesn't fall and make a noise."

They guided me into the shower, then stood and watched as the wool sweater and my trousers soaked up the water. The sweater gradually began to grow heavier and soon it felt like it was hanging down around my knees. As the sleeves soaked up the water they seemed

215

to stretch and gather around my wrists. My wool stockings and the low cut ski boots were soaked and one of the stockings dropped down around my ankle.

"Just stay there for a while, Dev. Enjoy it," Danielle said, sounding like she didn't mean a word. "Renee, we're going to take him down to the lobby. Then I want you to get my car and pick us up out front."

Paris suddenly got a large smile across his face. "Turn the hot water on."

"No, we don't need him screaming and waking the neighbors. We'll get him nice and wet, and then let him cool down outside." She half laughed.

"Maybe I'd better grab one of those softball bats from the office closet," Paris said, warming to the idea.

Danielle nodded. "Excellent idea, we'll let him soak a while longer before we go. Nice and warm for you, Dev?" she asked, then smiled, but kept the revolver pointed at me. I had no doubt she'd squeeze the trigger a lot faster than it would take me to step out of the shower and head butt her.

Ten minutes later Danielle reached in and turned off the shower. I was absolutely soaked and could feel the weight of the wet wool. Even tied behind my back I could sense that the skin on my hands had gone pruny from all the warm water.

"Help me get him out of here, Renee," she said. Then they guided me out of the tub and back into the hallway, my feet sloshed with every step. We waited by the front door to the condo. Danielle draped a bath towel over my shoulders, covering the wrists tied behind my back. I could hear the water dripping off of me and onto the carpet. Paris came back around the corner holding onto a softball bat and using the thing as a cane.

216

"Now we're going to go downstairs. One false move, one blink in the wrong direction and you'll disappoint a lot of women. Understand?" she said, then pressed the revolver into my crotch and smiled.

I nodded. "Yeah, completely."

"Good, let's get going."

Chapter Forty-Seven

We were waiting by the front door of the lobby. I was already shivering and we were still inside staring out into the darkness of the winter night. The wind was gusting audibly and waves of snow blew across the frozen garden outside. I noticed my skis stacked in a corner against the brick wall.

"Those are my skis there," I said. You could hear a chattering in my voice and I couldn't stop my body from shaking. My clothes were still dripping water and there was a puddle collecting around my feet.

"I don't think you'll be needing them any time soon," Danielle said. A pair of headlights suddenly stabbed through the darkness, and turned into the circular drive. As Paris pulled up to the front of the building gusts of snow seemed to flee before the headlights.

Danielle shoved the barrel of the revolver into the base of my spine. "Looks like your ride is here, let's go."

She stepped behind me and I had to shoulder the door open. The cold air hit me and I felt my lungs actually seize up for a moment. The wind ripped the bath towel off my shoulders and blew it into a snow drift. Danielle shoved the revolver harder into my back and we kept moving toward the car. I was having trouble walking.

"Jesus Christ," she groaned, then pushed the revolver into the base of my spine again. "Get moving."

Both our heads were down in a vain attempt to shield our face from the wind. We made it to the car and Danielle opened the rear door. I was shivering uncontrollably.

"Crawl in there on the floor," she directed.

I had trouble climbing in the car with my hands tied behind my back. I hoisted myself up on the seat and attempted to slide across. I was shivering so badly I couldn't control my movements.

"Come on, it's cold out here, damn it. Renee, give him a hand," she said and then leveled the revolver at me.

Paris reached over the seat, groaned, grabbed me by the collar and pulled me back along the seat then he half twisted me down toward the floor. I could hear water being squeezed onto the floor when he twisted my collar. Danielle jumped in and bounced her feet on top of me. She slammed the door closed and said, "God, turn up the heat and then head out toward Afton."

I couldn't stop shaking. I was so cold I was having trouble thinking. Afton. The St. Croix River Valley. The border between Minnesota and Wisconsin. Just a couple of small communities with lots of open farmland and not too many people around. I focused on my shivering.

"Wow, Dev, it's like having a vibrator on my feet. You must really be cold." She giggled.

"I'm, I'm freezing down here." I gasped. I couldn't stop shaking. My feet were numb and I could feel the

219

muscles in my thighs beginning to knot up from the cold.

"Good, but take your time or you'll ruin all our fun," Danielle said.

We drove for about a half hour, the last ten minutes or so we were off the interstate and traveling somewhere on a county road. I'd say the road was bumpy, maybe. That might have meant it was gravel, but I was shaking so badly I really couldn't tell.

"Right here looks perfect," Danielle said after a bit and Paris stopped the car. "Get out and give me a hand."

"What?" Paris said from the front seat.

"Renee, damn it, come on. He's shaking so bad he's half dead as it is."

"God damn it," Paris cursed and then continued complaining as he hobbled around the back of the car and opened the door. "God, my ankle's killing me, I'm going to have to go into urgent care tomorrow and get it checked out."

Danielle climbed out and said, "For God's sake, Renee. Just pull him out, will you? Here, give me the keys. I'll drive us back into town and take you to the emergency room. We'll get you checked out."

I felt someone grabbing my ankles, but I was so cold I couldn't tell if I was moving or not. "No, no, wait, please." I was shivering so badly I couldn't think of anything else to say.

My teeth were chattering. I couldn't stop my head from shaking. I was suddenly aware I was upright. My legs refused to work so the two of them dragged me out in front of the car and into the glare of the headlights. I was vaguely aware of the wind howling. Snow gusted and skittered across the country road, then disappeared off into the darkness and the flat, empty landscape.

With my hands tied behind my back my fingers could just make out the sodden wool already turning to ice.

Suddenly I was pushed from behind and tumbled head over heels into the snow. Deep snow and cold. Oh, so damn cold. I floundered, tried to get up, but couldn't and fell forward, head first, plowing deeper into the snow.

"Get up, Dev, come on, there's a warm house. See, just over there. Come on, it's only a couple of miles." Danielle laughed from somewhere far behind me. Then her voice seemed to grow distant and there was another sound, like the roar of an engine.

I heard Paris screaming her name. "Danielle, wait, don't. What do you think you're doing? Dan…"

In my dream Jimmy White was standing next to me. We were both staring at the ground, I had a slingshot in my hand and Mr. Graham was saying he was only going to ask us one more time. I was cold. God, I was so cold I was almost beginning to feel warm. "I, I didn't mean to. I didn't."

Then I heard Jimmy's voice. "It's okay."

Chapter Forty-Eight

It was the warm fleece blanket being draped over me that caused my eyes to flutter open. There was a gentle glow coming from the small light on the table next to the bed. The walls of the room looked to be a soft gray or maybe light blue. I couldn't really tell.

All I knew was, I wasn't in my bedroom and I sensed it wasn't a hospital room either. Well, unless the nurses had taken to wearing long sleeve flannel night gowns during their shift.

"Oh, sorry if I woke you. You're coming around. How are we feeling?"

"The blanket feels good, nice and warm," I said.

"I've got another one heating up in the dryer. Been keeping you warm for the past couple of hours." Her red hair was pulled back in a loose bun and she laid a hand on my forehead for a moment. Then she placed her fingers along the side of my neck checking my pulse.

"You cut it close, but I think you're gonna make it." She smiled. "Probably take it easy the next few days. How 'bout something warm? Maybe some homemade soup?"

"Ahhh, yeah, sure, that sounds good. Sue, how the hell did I get here?"

She turned at the sound of rustling just behind her. I caught the shadow of a figure getting up from a rocking chair. He stretched briefly, then put his arm around her shoulder and leaned into the light.

"You dumb shit," Jimmy White said and then smiled at me.

The look on my face must have said it all.

"Don't go passing out on me again, Dev. Christ almighty, I wasn't sure you were going to make it and you're a major pain in the ass to carry."

"Jimmy?"

"Yeah. Surprise, surprise," he said and shrugged.

"I thought you…Sue told me. Hell, I read your obituary in the paper, online. You're dead."

"Yeah, well, there you go, don't believe everything you read."

"What the…" I was speechless.

"Honey, maybe you should dish up that soup you mentioned. I'll get old 'Nanook of the North' here brought up to speed."

Sue nodded and left the room, closing the door behind her. Jimmy watched her go, then pulled the rocker a little closer to the bed and sat down. "Well, where to begin?"

"I know a little bit about it. I mean the collapse of the economy. From what I read it sounded like you got caught up in the real estate musical chairs and you just ended up hanging out there when all the music stopped."

"Partially correct. Except we found out later that Paris and Hedstrom had the thing wired from the get go. More of a ponzi scheme than anything else. Still, it was partially my fault for not doing more due diligence and really checking them out."

"But, the jumping off the bridge thing, your suicide. What the hell was that?"

"They cheated me and they cheated Sue along with a lot of other people. And then the bastards got away with it. I understood it was a risky business, but I played by the rules. Hell, most people do. But when you've got a guy who breaks the rules or makes up his own and then hangs you with the debt, that's just not right and it sure as hell shouldn't be legal. Did you read about their prosecution? Let me save you the time, there wasn't one. They weren't charged. Hell, they weren't even investigated."

"I get Paris, but how does Richard Hedstrom fit into all this?"

"That guy, Christ the two of them made a real pair. What one didn't think of the other did. They finally had a falling out over this last deal. That's why Paris set that fire."

"The fire at Casey's? You know about that?"

"I know about a lot of stuff, Dev. Even where some of the bodies are buried. I've been following your ass around for weeks. After you came over and talked to Sue she called me and I flew back here. You and I may not have kept in touch these last fifteen years, but I knew you'd keep poking around. I knew you went to Casey's and met with Paris. I watched you go there and I watched you leave. You were working for the Roxbury girl, right? The one with that big old house."

"Danielle? God, she's the one who left me out there to die, well, her and Paris. By the way she's not rich. At least, not anymore."

"Don't be too sure about that, Dev. I think she might be covered."

224

"What?"

"Not important. Look, the important thing here is that you're okay. I saw her drive off, but I couldn't follow and leave you. You would have been frozen solid in a couple of minutes."

"Now what? What are you going to do?"

"Me? Us? We'll be heading off somewhere now that things here have more or less been settled. I've been putting together our new life for the last seven years. Besides, we gotta move before Jimmy starts to really catch on."

"I met him, Jimmy. Nice kid, he reminded me of you, looks just like you at that age."

"Yeah, he was a little surprise. I'm supposed to be dead for two years and Sue suddenly shows up pregnant and then delivers a carbon copy of me, pardon the pun."

It suddenly dawned on me she had mentioned the kid was only five.

"What are you going to do?" I asked.

"Stick with our plan. Obviously, they never found my body. It's been seven years, now. They declared me dead about ten months ago, the insurance finally came through for Sue. Sue and Jimmy will be moving somewhere a little nicer, out of this climate. It's taken a while, but we're good to go."

"Someplace south then, warmer?"

Jimmy smiled. "You should probably get some sleep, man. Pretty busy night."

"I need to tell you something," I said then reached over and grabbed his wrist.

"This isn't a proposal is it? Can't it wait till morning?"

"No, it's long over due. You remember that time with the window, Mr. Graham and our slingshots?"

"When we were kids?" He looked surprised, no idea where I was going.

"Yeah, I never thanked you. I never had the balls to fess up. It's bugged me ever since."

"What?"

"I broke that window and you took the heat. Remember? Your folks grounded you for a good week and I just left you out there, hanging. I'm sorry, Jimmy. Sorry I let you down."

"Hell, Dev." He chuckled. "You're no smarter now than you were back then. I did it, my shot hit the window. I'm the one who broke the damn thing."

"You sure, because I think I was…"

"Dev, I'm dead sure." He smiled at that. "Honest, it was me. You didn't let me down then and you sure as hell didn't tonight. I couldn't have done this without you. You got me paid in full."

I looked at him, not sure what he meant.

Jimmy smiled, placed both his hands around mine. "Thanks, man. Of all people, you got the brass ones. Now, I have to get some sleep. We'll run you home in the morning. Sue will bring some soup in for you in a minute. Probably get another warm blanket for you too."

Chapter Forty-Nine

"Dev?" It was Jimmy. He was standing at the door to the little bedroom, leaning against the doorframe.

I opened my eyes, and waited for a second or two before my mind caught up to the surroundings. I half rolled over to look at him.

"You can wear these," he said, then tossed some jeans and a sweatshirt onto the bed. "Sue will be back in a few minutes, she's dropping Mr. Curious off at daycare. She's gotta get to work, I have a flight to catch, we can drop you home on the way."

"Yeah, oh, man," I said, crawling out of bed, "still a little tender on the fingers and toes." I looked at my hands, the fingers looked sunburned.

"Lucky you can even feel the damn things. Soaked like that, I wasn't kidding, you were maybe good for just a couple of minutes out there. That field and with the snow that came in last night, they wouldn't have found you till Memorial Day."

"Thank God you were following them."

"I wasn't," Jimmy said. "I was following you. I pulled into that scenic overlook just as you skied away. It was obvious where you were headed. I just watched

227

and waited. You do what I've been doing the last seven years, you learn some patience. Anyway, you better get dressed, Sue's back any minute," he said then left the room.

I climbed into the back seat of Sue's car, a non-descript gray Toyota. She was driving, Jimmy buckled up next to her in the passenger seat.

"Sue, you know you got a broken headlight? On your passenger side," I said and reached for the seatbelt. I was sitting next to the empty car seat.

They exchanged a quick glance that seemed to speak volumes.

"Sorry I don't have a jacket for you, Dev. Those boots okay?" Jimmy asked.

"Yeah, not to worry, I can feel the heat back here."

"You got a way to get into your place?"

"Yeah, spare key hidden by the porch."

I had a ton of questions to ask, but didn't know where to begin. I wasn't sure how much Sue knew or didn't know. Everyone was quiet driving down Robert Street. She cut over at the light on Concord, heading toward Wabasha. She drove across the Wabasha Bridge and into downtown, and then turned left on Kellogg to make her way up the hill. In the morning sun the dome of the Cathedral glowed imperiously from the top of the hill.

Jimmy and Sue were making small talk about his flight, little Jimmy's day care, what she was going to cook for dinner.

"There some way I can get in touch with you?" I asked.

They exchanged another one of those glances that spoke volumes. Then Jimmy turned half-way and looked at me in the back seat.

"Probably not the best idea, Dev. Please don't take it personal, but not now. Maybe give it thirty or forty years."

"That's a long damn time. I'd like to see you before then. I have no idea what happened last night. I mean to Danielle and Paris."

"I think the less you know the better. It's just best this way, Dev. Sue and I have seven years of living apart and getting back on our feet. Hope you won't be offended, but we've got too much time and heartbreak invested to change course now."

I nodded. I didn't like it, but I understood, sort of.

Sue drove past the Cathedral then took a right on Selby. We waited while two women crossed at the intersection with Western Ave. no doubt making their way toward Nina's and coffee.

"I'm just up here in the next block, on the right hand side. Next to that white house, mine's the one with the snow shovel on the front porch."

Sue pulled along the curb and stopped in front of my driveway. She didn't put the car in park, just kept her foot on the brake signaling this was going to be a short goodbye.

"Sue, thanks for taking care of me last night, and for taking care of this idiot."

Jimmy laughed, and held his hand out. We shook and I looked deep into his eyes.

"It's been too long, man. I'll let you get in touch with me, but make it a little sooner than thirty years. I'll get these boots back to Sue," I said.

"Don't, just keep them."

I nodded, said a final, "Thanks," and got out. I walked around the back of the car and up the three steps toward my porch.

"I doubt you'll hear anything more from Mr. Paris, Dev," Jimmy called from the car.

I turned to ask him something, but they were already pulling away.

Chapter Fifty

I put my fears aside and stepped into my own shower. It was warm, safe, I was the only one in the bathroom and I was still out of there in just under three minutes. I dressed in my own clothes. I called Louie to see if I could scam a ride down to the office. He didn't answer. I phoned Heidi next and got the same result. So I called a taxi and waited.

I still had my jacket on and was staring out the office window when Louie came in. I'd been doing pretty much the same thing for the better part of four hours. Nothing.

"Well, look who finally…you okay, Dev?"

"Yeah, just thinking."

"Well, that's it then, that's why I thought you looked so different, you were actually thinking," he said, then threw his jacket on the picnic table. "You didn't make any coffee?"

"What? No, I guess not. I'll take some if you're making it."

"You sure you're okay? Christ, you look like you just lost your best friend," Louie said, then started scooping coffee into the paper filter.

231

"Yeah, fine, don't worry. I'm going to take your advice, by the way."

"You are?" He sounded shocked. Then followed with, "Which advice are we talking about?"

"I put a call into Eddie Bendix, the guy at the insurance company. See if he's got any research or checking on job references he needs done. I could go for some dull work right about now."

"Plus, it pays," Louie said.

"Oh, yeah, there is that."

We drank some coffee. Louie was sitting on the edge of my desk, I was in my chair. We were both staring out the window when something caught our eye. We looked across the street, up on the third floor a figure strolled in front of the window and stopped to look down on the traffic. One of the sisters clad in a very small thong. She looked to be attaching the back of an earring.

"God, I wish she'd get that thing in and put her arms down," Louie said.

At which point she did exactly that. She continued to look down on the street a second or two longer before she drifted back into some darkened area of the apartment.

"Hopefully that was a sign of spring," Louie said.

"It's still January, Louie. We got a ways to go."

"One can always hope."

"Yeah."

I picked up a stack of a hundred files from Eddie Bendix the following day. "More of those when you're finished, Dev. We're gearing up a new section to deal with all the Affordable Care Act bullshit."

"I'll have these back to you in a couple of days," I said.

232

I did, as a matter of fact. I picked up another hundred files, and then another after that. When I dropped the third batch off Eddie called me into his office.

"Dev, not a reflection on your work, it's really helped, but we've put someone on staff who can handle this now, the reference checking. Hope you understand."

"To tell the truth, I was kind of wondering why you weren't doing it internally."

"We'll stay in touch," Eddie said. "Something's always coming up. Check is in the mail to you on Friday."

Chapter Fifty-One

It was Valentine's Day. Actually, it was the seventeenth of February, three days later when I phoned Heidi.

"Hello."

"Heidi, its Dev."

"I'm just between things, can I call you back?"

"Yeah, sure."

"Thanks, bye, bye, bye."

My phone rang a few minutes later. I answered it without looking and kept the binoculars up. Both sisters were strolling around the third floor across the street in various states of undress. A night of Heidi would serve as the perfect Grande Finale.

"That was fast. Is baby in need of some *special* attention tonight?" I said, then sat back and waited for Heidi to invite me over for a night of uncontrolled passion.

I heard the gum crack just before he yelled, "Haskell."

"Yes?" I tried to hide my disappointment by sounding overly sweet. I snapped my fingers a couple of times to get Louie's attention. He looked up from his laptop on the picnic table.

234

"Am I interrupting?" Manning sounded hopeful.

"Who is this?" I asked.

He ignored my question and said, "I wonder if you'd have time later this afternoon to stop in and see me."

"Is this just for a friendly chat or should I have my attorney present?" I asked.

Louie pointed at himself, nodded, raised his hand and gave me the okay sign.

"This is just a friendly little chat, no need for legal counsel."

"I'll bring him anyway. You name a time."

"I'd like nothing better than to see your smiling face at the end of today. Say four o'clock?"

"Four o'clock today?" I said in Louie's direction, he nodded back. "We'll be there."

Manning hung up.

"Any ideas?" Louie asked.

"No, nothing, unless those two sisters across the street reported us."

"In which case, Manning would probably be over here to view the scene of the crime."

"I know one thing, I'm giving Heidi's number a ring tone. I don't need Manning screwing up my social life."

We were five minutes early when Manning ushered us into the conference room.

"Damn it, forgot a file, give me just a minute, gentlemen," Manning said, then dashed down a hall.

"Not like him to forget something," Louie half whispered.

"You recognize this place?" I asked. It was the same room where we'd met with Manning last December along with that humorless psychologist Theobelle Sinn.

235

"Kind of hard to forget. I wonder where she's hiding?" Louie said then looked under the table.

"Here we go, have a seat, gentlemen. Please," Manning said then closed the door behind him. Louie and I sat down next to one another. Manning pulled a chair out directly across from us.

"Can I offer either of you some coffee?" he asked, standing behind his chair. He was definitely in his *'good cop'* mode.

"No thanks," Louie said.

I shook my head *'no'*.

"Very well, then. Let's get started. Shall we?" he said, then pulled his chair a little further back and sat down. He casually opened a fairly thick file. On the top of the file sat a black and white image, a head shot of some guy. As per Manning, the thing was upside down and I couldn't recognize who it was. And as per Manning I was sure he was gauging my reaction to the image.

Manning went through his usual introductory routine, the time, date, our location. He introduced me first, then Louie, adding that Louie was there, "In the capacity of legal representative."

"Now then, Mr. Haskell." Manning smiled at me. "I wonder if you would be able to identify this individual for me?" he said, then slid the black and white image out of his file and across the conference table toward me. The image was a copy from a printer, not a photograph and if I had to guess I'd say it had been enlarged from whatever the original had been. It was slightly blurry and clearly not a booking mug shot.

The guy could have been in his late forties or he could have been sixty. It was a full face, not what I'd call fat, but he could stand to lose a few pounds. Although it was a black and white copy the eyes looked

236

pale, I guessed they were blue. His hair was close cropped, grayed at the temples and thinning on top. The nose had a prominent bump and I figured it had been broken at least once. There were puffy bags under the eyes. I studied the image for a few moments and then shook my head. "I don't have any idea who that is."

Manning nodded and slid two more images over to me. Once again they looked to be enlarged copies from some sort of digital original. If I had to guess I'd say all three images were of the same individual and maybe taken over a span of ten or twenty years. Looking left to right the hair grew shorter, a little more gray and the face became a little heavier. Deeper lines ran along either side of the guy's face from his nose down to below his mouth. The bags under his eyes became more obvious. The nose was the same on all the images. I shook my head again. "I still don't have any idea who that is."

Manning nodded and reached back across the table. He gathered up the images and returned them to his file. "Let's talk about Renee Paris, shall we?"

"I don't know that I can tell you anything new," I said.

"Have you spoken with Mr. Paris since the afternoon you assaulted him in the kitchen of Casey's?"

"I have not had a meaningful conversation with Renee Paris since the afternoon I met with him at Casey's," I said, hoping that would satisfy Manning.

It didn't.

"You've not spoken to him since?"

"I have not," I lied.

Manning studied me for a very long moment. Like he knew my game and was just thinking of the best way to catch me in the act.

"What about Danielle Roxbury?"

237

"I think I drove past her home twice since our last conversation. I can't be sure of the dates, but it was sometime last December. On one of those occasions I got out of my car and rang her doorbell. No one answered. I have not phoned her. She has not phoned me."

Manning studied me again. "So you've not met with her."

"No."

"Nor contacted her."

"Correct."

"Has she contacted you, Dev?"

It was the first time I could remember that Manning called me Dev. I was more than a little worried.

"No, she has not contacted me and I have not tried to contact her, well except like I said, I drove past her house, twice."

"And rang her doorbell," he reminded me.

"Yes, and except for ringing her doorbell, the one she never answered."

"Do you have her phone number, have you called her?"

"The phone number I have for her is the same one I gave you last December. I presume it's still good, but I don't know that for sure. I have not called her. Here, you can check my phone if you want," I said. I pulled my cell phone out and set it on the table.

"We've already done that." Manning smiled. "Of course, you could have used another phone, maybe a pay phone or even Mr. Laufen's phone."

"Detective." Louie sounded genuinely annoyed. "I can assure you Mr. Haskell has not made any calls using my phone."

Manning smiled like maybe he had already checked Louie's number too.

"I didn't use Mr. Laufen's phone. I didn't attempt to call Danielle Roxbury on a pay phone. I didn't send her a telegram, an email, a text message or a carrier pigeon. I have not been in contact with the woman in any way, shape or form. The last phone conversation I had with Danielle Roxbury was sometime in December. I told her she should hire an attorney and she informed me that she was no longer in need of my services."

"Convenient," Manning muttered, but didn't say anything else.

My phone on the table suddenly rang. It played a few bars from the Blondie tune, '*Call Me*'.

"You kidding? I love Blondie." Manning seemed to step out of his cop role for a moment and gave a genuine smile.

The tune was at the '*designer sheets,*' point when it replayed.

"Go ahead and answer it." Manning nodded, curious. "We're pretty much finished here."

"Hi, Heidi. Look, I'm sort of busy, can I call you back?"

"No rush, I'm seeing someone, Denton."

"Okay, thanks, I'll call you later."

"Don't you even want to know?" she half screamed.

"Later," I said and hung up. "Just a lady friend." I smiled across the table at Manning.

"She didn't sound all that friendly just now," he said.

"Is there anything else, Detective?"

"No, thank you for your time, gentlemen. You're free to go. I'm sure you'll let me know should anything

239

develop on your end," Manning said, sounding like he didn't mean a word of it.

"You'll be the first we call," I said.

"Thank you," Louie and I said in unison then we stood up and fled the scene.

Chapter Fifty-Two

"Is it your turn or my turn?" Louie asked and pushed his glass toward Mike standing on the other side of the bar.

"God, I can't stand it, the two of you are like a couple of little old ladies. Just shut up, this round's on me," Mike said and left to refill our glasses.

It was a little before nine. We were seated at the end of the bar near the front door. There were maybe five other guys in The Spot. We were the only two talking.

"I knew the moment Manning sat down and opened the file with that image that it was Dick Head's picture. I hadn't seen the bastard for a few years, but it was him," Louie said, then followed up with a sip from his fresh drink.

"Why didn't you say something?"

He looked at me like I'd lost what was left of my mind. "Because the man didn't ask me, Dev. You don't go into those situations with the idea that you're going to volunteer information. It's painfully obvious you haven't learned that lesson."

"What are you talking about? What'd I do wrong this time?"

241

"You always want to play it too close to the edge. Say just one more thing to make your point and convince Manning. Only he's not going to be convinced, and that's where you always seem to get tripped up."

"Did I get tripped up this afternoon?"

"No," Louie said then took a small sip before he added, "for a change."

We closed The Spot. I took the back roads home and avoided any patrolling squad cars. After my Lincoln got totaled in that hit and run I had to buy a new car, at least it was new to me. A dark-green, 1997 Mercury Mountaineer, almost, but not quite old enough to be a classic. Probably quite a car in its day, back when 'W' had been in the White House. It got me where I wanted to go and at least the heater worked. That was an improvement.

The following morning I made my way down to the office around eleven. I was the first one in and put on a pot of coffee, then sipped and looked out the window. This was one of those February days where the sun was shining, the temperature was about two degrees above freezing and you had just a sliver of hope that spring wasn't too far behind. Of course, the temperature was bound to fall by the end of the week and bring ten to twelve inches of fresh snow along with it. But still, there was the beginning of hope.

I watched two women walking across the street. They looked to be dressed for exercise with fleece jackets, mittens, sort of tight sweatpants, walking shoes of a sort that looked pretty new. More hope for spring.

They were moving at a pretty good clip up Randolph in the direction of the hill. One of them made a disgusted face as they passed by The Spot, then she launched into some animated harangue, waving her arms around and had the other woman laughing. They passed my building without so much as a glance and kept moving.

I phoned Heidi, but she didn't answer. I figured she was still probably mad at me for not being interested in the latest details of whoever she was dating. I debated leaving a message and in the end just said, "Heidi, Dev, returning your call, give me a ring," and then hung up.

Louie's car suddenly pulled up against the curb across the street. He parked so his car was still part way into the bus stop area, even though the street was empty for at least a hundred feet in front of him. He quickly climbed out and rushed across the street, dodging traffic like he was in a desperate hurry to get to the bathroom.

It looked like he was wearing his blue suit again. Even from this distance and through the dirty window the suit appeared tired and wrinkled. I heard him clomping up the staircase and a moment later he burst into the office.

"You hear it on the news this morning?" he asked, then pulled a folded newspaper from his jacket pocket and tossed it onto my desk along with a couple of letters.

I glanced at the headline and looked up. "You're kidding me, there's already a budget overrun with the new ballpark?"

"Not that, you idiot, below the fold, bottom right. Recognize him?"

I flipped the paper over and looked at the image staring back at me. It was the same shot of Richard Hedstrom that Manning had shown us yesterday. The headline read, '*Remains Identified.*'

"Shit." I went on to read the three brief paragraphs below Hedstrom's photo. They said it had taken dental charts to identify what remained *of 'local St. Paul*

243

attorney and investor, Richard Hedstrom.' They made it sound like just his teeth had been found in the fire rubble at Casey's with no further speculation beyond that. No mention was made of Paris or Danielle. The article ended with the standard, *'Police are asking that anyone with information contact them at'* and then it gave a phone number and an email address.

I glanced up at Louie. "Is there anything else?"

"Not in the paper. I went through the thing twice, nothing. I caught a couple of seconds on public radio, but they didn't offer any more information."

"This is probably why Manning had us down there yesterday. He knew this was going to be in the paper today."

"Wow, you really are an investigator," Louie said. He sat down behind the picnic table, but kept his jacket on. "Figured you would want to see that right away."

"I don't know that it helps anything except that it drops a few more questions onto my plate."

"Such as?"

"I guess the same thing Manning's asking. What was Hedstrom doing there? Where the hell is Paris? And why the fire at Casey's in the first place?"

"Well, while you're pondering those basics you might want to check your mail there." He nodded at the envelopes he'd tossed on my desk.

"What the hell's this?" I asked.

"I'm guessing bills."

"What?" I asked, tearing open the envelopes. "You're kidding, I'm getting billed for them towing my car after that hit and run? Someone tried to kill me for God's sake." I said, looking up from the city invoice.

"I'm guessing that other one…"

"Metro Transit?" I asked, reading the return address. "Four hundred and fifty eight dollars to clean

244

up that bus bench? They're billing me? I don't believe this." I yelled a moment later.

"I think they have a number to call if you want to dispute the charges," Louie said.

Chapter Fifty-Three

I was at my desk with the binoculars up. The bird watching had been exceptionally good every morning this week with the sisters strutting their stuff across the way. It was almost Easter, the snow was more gone than not. Even at night when the temperature dropped back down it still remained above freezing. People were beginning to smile again. Cars were getting washed. Trees threatened to bud and tulips were beginning to push toward the surface. You could just feel the positive vibe returning to the saintly city.

I picked up on a figure strutting in front of the picture window on the third floor across the street. I redirected my attention from the two girls at the bus stop. I moved the binoculars up toward the picture window and focused. At first I thought one of the sisters was pregnant. Even worse, it turned out to be some guy with a beer belly sipping coffee and unfortunately clad in boxers. That was more than enough for me and I went to grab some coffee of my own.

My phone sang out, it was Heidi. I answered before Blondie got to the second stanza of the ring.

"Hello."

"Hi Dev, Heidi. I'm returning your call."

"My call?"

"From the other day. I called you. Apparently, you were so busy you couldn't talk to me. You called me, so now I'm calling you back."

"The other day? Heidi, that was six weeks ago."

"Get out of here, it couldn't have been."

"Guess again, it was. Matter of fact it was three days after Valentine's Day, the seventeenth, I remember."

"Whatever. Anyway, I'm calling you back. What did you want?" she said, suddenly sounding down. I had a pretty good idea where this was going. God knew I'd been here countless times before.

"Everything okay? How are things going with…"

"Don't mention his name."

"Dalton?"

"It was Denton, and if I never hear his name again it will be too soon."

This was where I was supposed to ask what happened. I had a better idea.

"Look it's been so long since we've been together, I'd love to take you out for dinner. You free tonight?"

"Actually, I just kind of feel like staying in."

"Okay, would I be imposing if I offered to come over and cook you dinner?"

"I suppose that would be okay, unless you wanted to just bring over some sort of take out."

"I could do that."

"Nothing fattening, no pizza, don't do White Castle again, that wasn't good. I'm out of wine. I suppose if you felt like it you could pick up some Prosecco?"

"No."

"What do you mean, no?"

247

I back tracked quickly. "I meant, let me surprise you. You just get comfy, I'll be there about six. That sound okay?"

"Make it seven, I've got yoga and then I'll want to shower."

Perfect. "Hey, you know what? Don't get dressed on my account. Just throw on a robe, get comfy, maybe stream in a chick flick if you want."

"You sure? You always say you hate those."

"No, not a problem, I'm sort of up for it. I'm just glad to finally be able to see you."

"God, I've been awful, haven't I? I'm sorry, I guess I've been kind of a bitch. I'll try and make it up to you."

Bingo!

"Not to worry, enjoy your workout, then relax and have a nice hot bath, maybe some bubbles. I'll be there around seven with dinner."

"Thanks, Dev, you're so sweet. See you then."

Perfect! It was going to be a well deserved great night.

Chapter Fifty-Four

"This isn't even the saddest part," Heidi sniffled. She was curled up in the far corner of her couch, legs tucked beneath her with a robe padlocked tightly around her waist. She clutched a paper dinner napkin. Apparently she had applied eye makeup after her hot bath. I knew that only because dark rivulets were running down either side of her face. Her glass of wine sat on the coffee table in front of her and remained largely untouched.

"I'm scared, Mommy. Is it getting dark outside?" A dog whined somewhere near the only bed in the pioneer cabin. The gorgeous female star blinked back tears and looked out the window at her young husband's gravestone under a large oak tree. There was about six minutes left in the movie and it was clear to me if the kid died I wasn't going to get any action. It would take Heidi the rest of the night to recover.

"Who digs a grave under a tree? What bullshit, all those roots, no one would do that."

"Please be quiet, you're wrecking this, Dev."

"But it's so stupid. Look at her she's not even dirty or sweaty after she supposedly carried that damn kid across the prairie for ten miles. Her hair isn't even…"

249

"Will you please shut the fuck up. You are wrecking this entire evening."

"Are you kidding? I brought dinner and thought you'd want…"

"Out," she said and pointed toward the front door. She hit the pause button and glared at me through red, puffy eyes. "You have ruined the mood, Dev. Why don't you just go to some sleazy bar and watch the hockey game or something?"

Actually, at this stage that didn't sound half bad.

"Now, I'm going to have to rewind this and if you say anything else you are so out of here. It's just heartbreaking she has to dig her little boy's grave all by herself."

"What?"

"I said she has to dig the grave by herself. Yes, Dev, under the big tree, with all the roots. Then she cries on top of the grave for days on end and practically starves, you never even know if she recovers." She made a face and shook her head as she said it, mimicking me.

"You mean you've seen this movie before?"

"You kidding? I love it." Then she pushed the rewind button, based on the digital counter that was displayed she rewound thirty minutes that I'd just suffered through. She blew her nose, then settled in for a fresh cry. The rewind had stopped right when the mom was about to shoot the favorite horse and then carry the kid for ten miles.

"Maybe we should just climb into bed and express our feelings in a little more physical…"

"Get out," she half screamed and pointed toward the door.

I raised my hands in surrender and rose from my chair. "It's been real, Heidi, catch you another night." I

250

walked toward the door and kissed her on the top of the head. I slowed for a couple of steps, hoping she'd come to her senses. She didn't. As I opened the door she hit the play button and began sniffling anew. Mommy was just about to pull the trigger and shoot the horse.

By the time I climbed on my stool at The Spot, Mike had drawn a Mankato ale for me and pushed it across the bar. "Working tonight?"

"Unsuccessfully." I nodded and took a sip.

There were two flat screens mounted up by the ceiling at either end of the bar. Both had a news station on, but the sound was off. I think it was Leonard Cohen I heard moaning on the jukebox. I just couldn't seem to catch a break tonight.

"You been busy, Dev? Haven't seen you around for awhile." Mike was washing pint beer glasses, two at a time. There was a wet sink, a soap sink, a rinse sink, and then a drying board. He sloshed both glasses in each sink a couple of times, then set them on the drying board. He had to bend over then move sideways about four steps to complete the entire process.

He'd maybe washed about twenty glasses and was making small talk that I hadn't been following. I was still half wondering what sort of idiot would attempt to dig a grave right beneath a giant oak tree. I glanced up at the flat screen. The image was a couple of squad cars and an ambulance. Two guys were rolling a stretcher with a body bag strapped onto it into the back of the ambulance. The scene looked to be out in the middle of nowhere. A large, flat, muddy field stretched out for miles with row after row of what looked like corn stalks that had been cut down last fall. There was still a fair amount of snow in the drainage ditch between the road and the corn field. I couldn't decide which was worse, the muddy field, Leonard Cohen or Heidi's movie. The night was a bust. I finished my beer and went home.

Chapter Fifty-Five

It was the end of the week and I was back sitting in the office in mid-afternoon. I'd been investigating work disability scammers for Eddie Bendix. I'd photographed a young lawyer the other day wearing a neck brace and using a walker to hobble around town. This morning at a little after six, I photographed the same young lawyer exiting his girlfriend's apartment and running to his car at the far end of her parking lot. Eddie was paying me twenty percent on these cases.

After tailing the couple for the better part of the evening I'd been parked on the street for most of the night. It had been worth the wait, but I was on my third cup of coffee and trying to stay awake when Louie strolled in.

"Coffee?"

"Yeah, I was on a stake-out all last night. I'm dragging."

"Sounds sinister."

"It was. There's a lawyer involved."

"Anyone I know?" He'd stopped in mid-stride toward the coffee pot.

253

"I doubt it, young kid just out of law school. Faking neck and back injuries to scam the insurance company."

"Your insurance pal Bendix?"

I nodded then glanced across the street to the third floor.

"Anything happening over there?" Louie asked.

"No, as a matter of fact, God I hope they haven't moved," I said.

"You hear the news?" Louie said.

Probably not. To be honest, I've been focused on these insurance scammers, I'm working five of them. Well, after last night probably down to four."

"Renee Paris. They found him."

"You're kidding, now what's he done?"

Louie shook his head. "They found him down in some drainage ditch out in Afton. I guess he'd been dead for awhile, buried under the snow. Some power line crew came across his body the other day. They just came out with the identification this morning."

The news report I'd glanced up at the other night when I was in The Spot flashed across my mind.

"God only knows what that bastard was doing out there on a deserted country road."

"Maybe he was looking for an investment opportunity," I said.

"In a drainage ditch?" Louie shook his head.

"What?"

"They figure he got hit by a car and landed there. Doesn't make a lot of sense. 'Course, the list is long and includes some well connected folks who would have loved to run over that guy, including your girlfriend, Danielle Roxbury. That's Washington County out there, I'd guess the cops probably looked up and down the road, didn't see a car, and called the case

254

closed. Hey, give me a yell if anything happens across the street," Louie said, then turned on his laptop.

I nodded, but I was thinking of the broken headlight on Sue White's car that morning a few months back. Then back to the night before, a snowy, freezing cold night. I remembered I thought the road was bumpy, but I was freezing and shaking so badly I couldn't really tell. Danielle told Paris to drag me out of the car. The wind was howling and the snow was blowing across the road. I was so cold, that's what I really remember, so damn cold. It had been bright in the headlights and that field seemed to just go on forever and ever...

"Oh, hey, some fan mail for you, too." Louie said and sailed a post card across my desk. It landed upside down, only my address was written on the back, no message. I flipped the card over and stared at the image of a slingshot. I flipped the card back over to check the postmark but it was smeared and unreadable.

"Are they up there?" Louie was standing at my side. He'd picked up the binoculars and dialed them in on the apartment window across the street. "Damn it, I must have just missed them. You were so focused I knew something was up. Oh, well, at least they're still up there," he said and went back to his laptop.

Chapter Fifty-Six

I had a rematch planned with Heidi tonight. I was pulling out all the stops, flowers, Thai take out, her favorite little pastry for dessert and Prosecco. I didn't care, it had become a matter of urgency. On the way over to Heidi's I'd picked up a small gift for Jimmy White, little Jimmy. I wasn't due at Heidi's for another hour and I figured what kid doesn't like Play Dough?

I turned the corner and pulled in front of the house. It was still the soft gray exterior, but all the white trim looked freshly painted. The door looked to have a fresh coat of that Fire Engine Red. Then there was the For Sale sign in the front yard, which might explain the freshly painted trim.

I rang the doorbell and peeked in the front picture window, the living room was empty, not so much as a dust bunny on the floor. Peeking in the bedroom window revealed the same result, complete and total emptiness.

I sat in my car and dialed the agent's number from off the sign.

"This is Kevin," he answered after a couple of rings.

I read Sue White's address to him off the front of the house and told him I might be interested.

"That's a very motivated seller and that property is priced to move. It's a great location, school just three blocks away, stable area, not too many turnovers pop up in that neighborhood."

"How long has it been on the market?"

"I've had that listing for maybe ten days, we're just coming into the season and after the long winter I don't expect it to be available for much longer."

"Where did they move to?"

"To tell you the truth, I don't know. I'm actually dealing with an attorney who represents the owner. They seem pretty tight lipped. That usually suggests a death or something. But it's been inspected. I've got the Truth in Housing report. Now the furnace is only four years old…"

Chapter Fifty-Seven

"**Okay, relax, will you?** Apology accepted. The flowers are beautiful, Dev, and thanks for bringing these bottles of Prosecco. Mmm-mmm, God, I just love Thai, don't you?"

"Yeah, Heidi, I do. Hey, can I ask you a sort of business question?"

"Sure," she said, then kind of partially turned her head and asked, "What's up?"

"Just a general question. I'm trying to get a handle on a guy. If you were a real estate sort of developer kind of guy and you'd taken a pounding in the crash…"

"Virtually everyone did, Dev," she said then filled her glass.

"Yeah, okay, so if you could choose any area of the country, any city, where would be the best place to go to for a fresh start?"

"That depends," she said, holding her glass and watching as the bubbles rose to the top.

"Depends on?"

"Well, are you talking commercial or residential?"

"I'm pretty sure commercial."

"Okay, commercial. Then it depends sort of on when. If you started or maybe we should say, restarted in 2007 or eight you might go to the usual places. L.A., maybe Seattle, Charleston, possibly outside D.C. somewhere, although D.C. would take really deep pockets right out of the starting gate. Another place, again we're talking commercial would be Vegas, the housing end of things was bad, but commercial hung on. But, if you didn't go right after the crash, maybe waited till 2010 or so, actually no romance, but North Dakota could be a big possibility."

"I don't think North Dakota would be the place."

"Just depends, I guess. You're not having any?" Heidi asked and held her glass out to be refilled.

"I'm pacing myself. Hey, I got one of your favorite desserts..."

"You are such a sweetie," she said, then flared her eyes in my direction.

I think I was more dead than alive when I woke. Over the course of the evening I had become a fan of Prosecco, at least when Heidi drank the better part of two bottles and then turned her undivided attention toward me. She lay next to me, groaning out another one of her deep Prosecco snores. We'd used her Jacuzzi, the top of her dresser and from the looks of things a number of different angles in her bed. She laid beside me, crossways across the bed, wearing a very contented look and one high heeled, black, knee high boot. It was a little after four in the morning when I heard my cell phone ring.

Ting-a-ling, ting-a-ling, ting-a-ling.

I was searching for my jeans. My cell was in the pocket. I followed the ringing noise and found my jeans right where Heidi tore them off out in the hallway.

As I answered I looked back in at Heidi. She was illuminated by the light coming from the scented candles still flickering in the bathroom. Her skin glowed almost iridescent in the soft light and contrasted beautifully with the recent jet black dye job on her hair. Her sleep seemed unfazed by my phone ringing.

"Hello."

"Mmm-mmm, this wouldn't happen to be Haskell Investigations, would it?" Danielle's sexy voice asked.

I paused for a moment, then said, "No, sorry, you have the wrong number," and hung up.

The End

Thanks for taking the time to read <u>Ting-A-Ling</u>. If you enjoyed Dev's adventure please tell 2-300 of your closest friends. Then check out the free sample of <u>Crickett</u> just after the list of all my titles available on Amazon.

Baby Grand

Chow For Now

Slow, Slow, Quick, Quick

Merlot

Finders Keepers

End of the Line

The following titles comprise the Dev Haskell series;

Russian Roulette: Case 1

Mr. Swirlee: Case 2

Bite Me: Case 3

Bombshell: Case 4

Tutti Frutti: Case 5

Last Shot: Case 6
Ting-A-Ling: Case 7
Cricket: Case 8
Bulldog: Case 9
Twinkle Toes
(A Dev Haskell short mystery)
Irish Dukes (Fight Card Series)
Written under the pseudonym Jack Tunney

Visit http://www.mikefaricy.com
Email; mikefaricyauthor@gmail.com
Twitter; @mikefaricybooks
On Facebook; Mike Faricy Books *and* Dev Haskell.

Crickett is the **EIGHTH** mystery in the highly entertaining Dev Haskell Private Investigator mystery series.

When the city's laziest Private Investigator Dev Haskell spots his old flame Karen Riley in The Spot bar, she's changed--for one thing she's no longer Karen Riley, now she's Crickett, and then there's the stroller with ten month old Oliver. Dev hangs on and does the math: ten months plus nine months equals when?

It seems Crickett's sometime lover Daryl has been caught in possession of some drugs, and she thinks they may have been planted on him. But five million dollars worth? Tough to hide that much in your pocket. Dev starts looking under rocks and quickly uncovers local crime lord Tubby Gustafson and his psychopathic enforcer, Bulldog. Things seem to go downhill rather quickly from there as Dev finds himself literally running for his life.

Crickett is a hilariously entertaining hard-boiled mystery, with just enough chills to keep you on the edge of your seat. A delightful read with a heavy dose of corner cutting and misbehavior to go with the beverage of your choice. Hope you enjoy the read.

Crickett
Mike Faricy

<u>Chapter One</u>

I dropped into The Spot for only one, four hours ago. Just as I signaled Mike for another, I caught sight of her walking in the side door. Karen Riley hadn't changed much in a year and a half. She did seem to bounce a little more enticingly as she came around the bar, of course that was before I saw the stroller with the baby. Two serious drinkers at the end of the bar had to move their stools so she could get past and they didn't look too happy about the interruption.

On our last night out she was staggering after drinking two bottles of pink champagne, she slipped getting into my car. As her skirt rose up around her waist she looked over her shoulder at me, licked her lips then said, "Maybe you'd like to give a girl a hand?"

I was only too willing to lend a helping grope.

Amazingly, the ride home had been uneventful, but only because I was able to fend Karen off despite her protestations. Before we'd driven a block she'd slipped her skirt off and tossed it onto the spare tire in the back seat. More than once I had to physically keep her at bay as we raced toward her house.

"Just pull over and let's do it, Dev. Come on," she sighed then ripped her blouse open.

We were only four minutes away from her place. I figured I could hang on, but sped up all the same. She seemed to settle down as I screeched around the corner onto her street. I pulled to the curb in front of her place, jumped out then quickly walked around to open her door.

It had all the makings of a night to remember and I rubbed my hands in delicious anticipation. As I opened the passenger door her purse fell to the ground, followed by her gorgeous legs swinging invitingly onto the sidewalk in a very unlady-like pose. She looked up at me with a glassy stare, but I don't think she saw me. Fortunately, at a little after three in the morning no one would be around to notice her thong attire. I stuffed a handful of items back into her purse then picked up a discarded red heel from the curb. Halfway along her stagger toward the front door she kicked the other shoe into the garden. She let her blouse fall to the ground just before the front steps. I stopped to retrieve it juggling her purse and the heels.

"It's been real, later baby," she slurred just as I heard the front door click open and she staggered inside. I clutched everything in my arms and hurried up the porch steps. I had five feet to go when she slammed the door closed behind her, stumbled into the middle of the living room then passed out on the floor.

I could see her through the front window, lying face down on the carpeted floor, wearing just her thong and a gold necklace, out cold. I rang the doorbell repeatedly. I pounded on the locked door then frantically searched around the porch for a nonexistent key. She remained dead to the world.

A clap of thunder brought me to my senses. I carried her shoes, purse and blouse back to my car. I tossed them on top of her skirt and the spare tire just as the rain began to pour down.

I don't know, maybe it was karma, bad karma I guess. I was back over there the following afternoon shampooing her living room rug and not having much luck removing the pink champagne stain.

Pasty looking Karen didn't seem to be in the best of moods stretched out on her living room couch. A blue terricloth robe was cinched tightly around her waist hiding any semblance of her figure and eliminating my hope of a *'thank you'*. She had an ice pack on her head, a box of Kleenex on her lap and occasionally sipped from a glass of 7-Up. When she spoke it was only to give me further rug cleaning directions or swear that she would never, ever drink pink champagne again.

I came back to reality as she forced the stroller around a table, flashed a smile in my direction then charged toward me pushing a wide-eyed little boy. The words *'Paternity Suit'* suddenly screamed in my head. I wasn't sure if it was the stroller with all the toys or the gigantic diaper bag that made her look like she was getting ready to set up a campsite.

"Well, well, well, Dev Haskell. I thought I might find you here," she said then proceeded to hoist the diaper bag onto the bar.

I had to clear my throat a couple of times before I could find my voice. "Great to see you again, Karen," I lied. "Who is this little guy?" I asked then gripped the edge of the bar and waited for the shotgun blast.

"This is our little Oliver, ten months. Oh, and just so you know, I've changed my name. Now I'm Crickett."

265

I felt light headed as the color drained from my face. I was too stunned to do the math in my head, nine months plus ten months before that equals when?

"Oh, Jesus, Dev calm down. God, look at you, you're pale as a ghost. Are you gonna be okay? It's Daryl and me, he's my boyfriend."

I still wasn't seeing anything funny in my honest mistake, but I faked it. "Well congratulations, Kar… I mean, Crickett. And aren't you the handsome little devil," I said looking down, actually he kind of was. I felt my heart slowing back down to normal. "What's with the Crickett name change?"

"Oh, Karen was just, I don't know, so proper, so churchy. Crickett is more me, more of my persona."

'Persona,' I thought. "Can I get you something?"

Mike strolled up and studied her from across the bar.

"Gee, thanks, but I better not. Course on second thought, maybe just a double Bombay Safire martini and two olives," she said all the while staring at Oliver. She shrugged her shoulders, shook her head back and forth and made a strange face at the baby.

"You want a bag of beer nuts or maybe some pork rinds for the little guy?" I asked.

"Ahhh, no I don't think so and his name's Oliver, Dev. If he gets hungry I'll just feed him. Yes, Oliver you're growing up to be a great big boy, aren't you? Yes, yes mommy's little moose." She sort of squeaked out the word 'moose' and the serious drinkers who'd had to move their stools glanced down the bar.

We chatted for a bit. At least I tried to chat. Crickett was busy making faces at Oliver and sipping her martini. She drained the glass, pushed it across the bar signaling for another, then turned toward me and thrust her chest out to take control of the conversation.

266

"Daryl and I need your help. It's kind of embarrassing, but I figured you're used to it."

"Being embarrassed?"

She nodded then said, "Yeah, you know the sort of situations you seem to get yourself into. Remember when you had that crazy woman who tried to kill you?"

"Which one, there've been more than a couple?"

She nodded like that sounded perfectly logical. "Well, of course I'd like to hear their side. Thanks," she said to Mike as he slid another filled to the rim martini in front of her.

"So what happened?"

She took a deep breath, a healthy sip then said, "Daryl was arrested, and our attorney said he should try to make a deal, only he didn't do anything."

I nodded like this made sense. Actually, in my line of work it sort of did.

Crickett looked around, then leaned forward and half whispered. "He was arrested with some drugs in his possession. Only he didn't know they were in his possession."

"Did someone plant them on him?"

"Sort of."

"How much are we talking about?"

"They said five million, at least that's the figure from the DEA, but I'm thinking they trumped it up. You know how they are."

"Even so, five million? That's not exactly an amount you can hide in your jacket pocket."

Oliver began to fuss at this point, and I half wondered if he somehow understood the gravity of his father's situation.

"Oh God, he can't be hungry. I'll tell you, all he does is eat," Crickett said. She didn't look all that thrilled as she lifted Oliver out of his stroller and onto

267

her lap. Even I had to admit, for ten months he was a pretty big guy.

"Do you want to grab that booth in the back so you can have little more privacy?"

"Oh honestly, it's completely natural, Dev, it's why God gave them to us," she said then pulled her top up, exposed her left breast and flashed a smile in my direction. It looked a lot larger than I remembered, and I stared while she took another healthy sip of her martini. Little Oliver clamped on the moment she set her glass down. Once attached, he turned his head and gave me a look as if to say, *'See what I got and you can't have any.'* The drinkers at the end of the bar suddenly looked a lot happier, stared for a long moment then ordered another round.

Chapter Two

Crickett went on to explain her boyfriend's predicament while little Oliver remained firmly attached. I suspected, given his male genes that he was just showing off, possession being nine-tenths of the law.

"So that's pretty much it. He just thought he was helping out a friend, driving this van into the parking ramp. They have him on video the entire way."

"The police?"

She nodded. "Yeah, I haven't actually seen the thing. I guess the video is like fifteen minutes long, including his arrest. It's just so obvious it was all a set up."

"Well, yeah, but he was arrested in possession of the van and there was five-million dollars worth of drugs in the thing. I'm guessing you don't hide that much in the glove compartment."

"Apparently they were all stacked up on a pallet in the back. Actually, two pallets I guess, but there was a tarp over them so he didn't really know. Anyway, we're going to dispute the five-million figure. I think it sounds high."

"Jesus. Who owns the van?"

269

"It was a rental."

"Who rented it?"

"Well, I guess it was supposed to be rented, but actually it was sort of just taken."

"You mean stolen?"

She gave a nonchalant nod then adjusted Oliver who seemed to be contentedly sleeping and still latched to mommy. The little glutton opened his eyes for a brief moment and shot me another glance that suggested *'Don't even think about it.'* Then he snuggled in closer and drifted back asleep.

"Did Daryl steal the van?" I asked.

"Well, that's what the police are saying. It's one of the charges against him. But the keys were under the floor mat so he just got in and drove off."

"And he was going to deliver this van to a parking ramp?"

She nodded like this made perfect sense.

Daryl wasn't sounding like the brightest bulb on the tree. His credibility was becoming an issue with me and I hadn't even met the guy.

"So what about the friend he was helping? Was he arrested too?"

"Not exactly. See, that's sort of the problem or at least one of the problems. We can't seem to find him. No one knows where he is, and then Daryl got this warning not to cooperate with the police." She leaned forward, glanced around cautiously, and whispered. "They said if he cooperated, Oliver and I would be killed."

Little Oliver suddenly began to suck viciously.

"Who's *'they'*?"

"We don't know. I'm guessing the drug people, but I don't have any names."

270

"The drug people." I wasn't sure where to begin. Every statement seemed to raise a half dozen common sense questions. Not the least of which was *'Could Daryl really be this stupid?'*

"Honestly, Crickett, I'm not sure what I can do here. Do you have a lawyer?"

She nodded. "We have a public defender, but she's really busy. She's the one who told Daryl to make a deal."

"Was she aware of the threat on your life?"

"Yeah, Daryl told her about it, but she said it didn't seem credible."

"Not credible? How would she know? What's her name?"

"Daphne..."

I waited for the bomb to drop, if it was Daphne Cochrane, I knew her as Daft, but had called her less charitable things. A few years back she had briefly been my court appointed public defender. I dropped her the moment she suggested I plead guilty to a murder charge. She was an eternally unhappy, impressed with herself, Ivy League, condescending witch who....

"Cochrane. Daphne Cochrane. She seems very smart."

'Yeah, and she'd be only too happy to tell you how very smart she is,' I thought.

"Do you know her?" Crickett asked.

"Not really," I said and let it go at that.

"I was wondering if maybe you could, you know, do some investigation or something so they drop the charges against Daryl."

"Crickett, did you talk to your lawyer, Daphne about this? Clear it with her?"

"She's sort of busy and well, like I said, she wants Daryl to cooperate with the police and hopefully he can

271

get some kind of deal. You know a reduced sentence and stuff. I just don't know."

I did know and if the threat to harm Crickett and baby Oliver was even halfway credible there was a good chance they would be killed and then once Daryl knew they were dead whoever was behind their murder would have him killed, too.

"I think you should request protection for starters. Tell your lawyer, Daphne that these folks aren't fooling around. If Daryl is going to cooperate, you two have to be safe. These drug folks aren't kidding. That size of a drug bust, five million, you've most likely got some pretty angry bad guys out there right about now. She can't just dismiss your concern. If she does then you should go straight to her boss."

"Yeah. I don't know it all seems so complicated."

"Complicated? Crickett, these are serious charges. He could be looking at twenty years."

"Daphne thought more like twenty-five, but she said he could get out in fifteen with good behavior." She said sounding like that was a really positive development.

"Fifteen years is still a lot, particularly if he's innocent."

"I suppose. But if you did some investigating then you could tell the police he's innocent, they'd let him go, he wouldn't have to cooperate and we would be safe," she said then half pulled little Oliver off the feed bag.

He quickly reattached himself.

"Crickett, I can look into some basics, maybe talk to the police, but your best bet is getting some protection and like I said, if your attorney doesn't want to do that maybe call her boss or ask for someone else to represent you."

"So you won't check? You won't investigate?"

"No, I mean, yes. I'll at least check on some of the basics. But let me be honest, based on what you've told me, this is what's referred to as an open and shut case. Even if we can prove Daryl is innocent..."

"Oh, I guess he most likely is, maybe."

Not the sort of ringing endorsement I would have hoped for. "Well, we still have an uphill fight on our hands, not only to prove he's innocent, but to get the charges against him dropped. And, look I'm willing to help, I'll do some initial checking, but at some point I'll have to charge you and this could get expensive very quickly."

She nodded like it was no big thing then said, "Okay, how soon before you can start your investigation?"

An image flashed across my mind. Crickett lying on her couch in that dreadful blue terri-cloth robe while I worked at mission impossible, attempting to shampoo two bottles worth of pink champagne out of her living-room carpet.

"I'll see if I can interview Daryl tomorrow. Let me get some general information from you first," I said and pulled one of the envelopes out of my back pocket so I could write some notes on the thing.

Chapter Three

"Yeah, and that's not the worst of it. The van was stolen," I said to Louie. He's my attorney. We share an office along with a number of wasted nights and some pretty vicious hangovers.

Louie leaned back in his office chair and put his feet up on the picnic table that served as his desk.

I continued to look through my binoculars into the third-floor apartment across the street hoping to spot one of the women who lived there. I wasn't having much luck.

"The van was stolen?"

"Yeah, like I said it get's worse. His pal told him the keys were under the floor mat. Innocent idiot Daryl Bergstrom drives off in the thing with two pallets of cocaine bricks sitting in the back under a tarp. He drives to a downtown parking ramp and apparently never questions any of this. Crickett said some pal paid him a hundred bucks to leave the van in the parking ramp. The cops have him on tape from the moment he gets in the van until his arrest in the parking ramp. I talked to someone down there and I'll see the tape tomorrow, but they've got this jackass nailed a hundred ways to Sunday."

"And someone is threatening your ex and her baby?"

"Ex is maybe too strong a term, we weren't together long enough to rate that title."

"She dumped you?"

"More like a mutual lack of interest. Although doing the math she must have been seeing this Daryl character at the same time. To tell you the truth, I'm guessing I was the dalliance or maybe a brief interruption and he was the steady boyfriend."

"When are you going to see this guy?"

"Tomorrow, right after I watch the surveillance video of him taking the van and then driving it into the parking ramp."

"It sure sounds like a setup. The cops are there filming, just waiting for someone to show up and drive off in the thing," Louie shook his head in disbelief.

"I'm guessing whoever the pal was with the hundred bucks, he knew what was going down or had some awfully strong suspicions. The cops weren't just filming, apparently they had a tracking device planted on the van, as well. Of course they've also got this numbskull on the parking ramp security cameras. Oh, and one of their undercover officers follows him into the ramp and parks about four spaces away on the same level."

"And he's clueless?"

"Apparently. Yeah, it's a setup, I think there's a good chance my guy is innocent of any drug offense along with guilty of being really stupid. But, that doesn't alter the facts and the facts are not in his favor, at least from what I can see."

Louie shook his head, then drained his glass and pushed it across the picnic table toward me. "After all that, I could use a little more to soothe my nerves."

I put the binoculars down on the window sill, poured a good inch into his glass and capped the fifth of Jameson.

"Not having any?"

"I gotta go to some fundraiser tonight with Heidi and be on my best behavior."

"Fundraiser?"

"I don't know, some political thing. Anyway, it usually works in my favor. I'll be her designated driver while she hob knobs with the *'Swells'*. Oh, get this, just in case things aren't bad enough for this Daryl dude, guess who's representing him?"

Louie took a sip and shrugged.

"Daft."

"Cochrane? Daphne Cochrane? God, poor bastard doesn't have a snowball's chance in hell. I hope you advised your lady friend to get another lawyer."

"Yeah, I did, but I think it just went in one ear and out the other."

"Mind if I make a suggestion?" Louie said then drained his glass. "He needs to cooperate, give his pal's name to the cops, hell, they probably already know who it is. Then he needs to get away from Daft. She'll get him sentenced to twenty years, killed, or both. I'll represent him pro bono if need be, but get him away from her, she shouldn't even be practicing."

"That's big of you."

"The M.O. fits in with my usual band of idiots. I can use the publicity and it won't cost me anything more than a little of my time."

"I'll pass it on," I said, then picked up the binoculars to resume my futile quest.

Chapter Four

I was seated at Heidi's kitchen counter paging through some dreadfully trashy magazine full of makeup tips and an expose on a Hollywood star I'd never, ever heard of. I'd been sitting there for the past half hour while Heidi tried on a dozen different outfits. All the while she was racing back and forth between her walk-in closet and the full length mirror in her bedroom she called to me. "I'll just be another minute."

"No rush."

"Almost ready," she called five minutes later.

"No problem, take your time."

She carried two different outfits on hangers from the closet then held them in front of her while she stood staring at the large mirror. I could hear her mumbling, "Oh, I don't know."

Truth be told, she looked fabulous in everything she'd tried on. She could have gone to the event in cut-offs and a T-shirt and still have been the most attractive woman there. But, painful past experience had taught me to keep my opinion to myself at this particular moment.

She strolled into the kitchen fifteen minutes later hooking an earring and looking like a million bucks. "What do you think?" she asked.

It's one of those questions like *'Does this dress make my ass look fat?'* or *'How old do you think I am?'* You're juggling a grenade and hoping the pin wouldn't fall out.

"I don't think you should wear that. It makes you look stunningly beautiful and every guy there will be hitting on you. I better go back home and get my gun."

"Stop, you're just saying that."

"Beautiful, Heidi, really nice." I was telling the truth.

"You don't think it's showing too much cleavage? I don't know, maybe I should wear a different bra."

"I think you're asking the wrong guy. I got an idea, let's skip this fundraiser and I'll send them a check for a hundred bucks. We'll stay here, just the two of us, and your wine glass will never be empty."

"Yeah, you'd love it. That's my going rate a measly hundred bucks?"

"Actually, I would love to stay here, and I'm sure my personal check would be acceptable."

"Hmm-mmm, too bad, come on we better get going. We're already late," she said making it sound like I had something to do with the tardy departure.

We made the short drive to downtown St. Paul and I pulled into the valet parking lane. I figured parking would probably run me twenty bucks, and we weren't even inside. The eighteen-year-old valet opened the passenger door for Heidi, then stood and stared at her with a ravenous look on his baby face. Apparently he agreed with me. He came to his senses after a long moment and walked over to me. "Man, I don't believe it, just like Walter White," he said as I handed him the keys to my Pontiac Aztek.

"It's been giving me a little trouble lately," I said failing to mention it had been a pain for the past ten months. He was still trying to start it when we walked into the reception area.

"Well, Heidi. My, my, aren't we looking grand," some guy said then planted a lingering kiss on her cheek. "Here, will a white do?" he asked and handed her one of the two glasses of wine he was carrying.

"Burt, how sweet," she cooed. "Say, I'd like you to meet a friend of mine, Dev Haskell. Dev, meet Burt," Heidi giggled.

Burt nodded and extended his hand. As we shook, he sort of half turned and cut me off. "Heidi, I wonder if I could have a private momentito. If you'd excuse us for just a bit, Dan," he said over his shoulder then hurried her off to a corner explaining some sort of involved thing I apparently wouldn't be able to comprehend.

I made my way to the bar, got a lite beer in a bottle for eight dollars and began to mingle. The fundraiser had a bar set up in all four corners of the large, chandeliered ballroom. None of them offered a decent beer, but then these were *'The Swells'* and I was out of my usual drinking element. I figured there might be a good three hundred plus people milling around paying exorbitant drink prices and trying to look interesting. I recognized a few people, but no one I really wanted to talk to. I couldn't see Heidi anywhere, but a casual glance around confirmed she would be the most attractive woman in attendance.

I finished my lousy beer and got another. I caught Heidi from across the room involved in an animated conversation with two guys, neither one Burt. I decided to stay away and wandered over to the hors d'oeuvres table. I could have saved the effort.

Apparently this was some sort of gluten free, vegan group. Not so much as a Dorito, cocktail wiener, or a meatball to save my soul. Most of the food trays were already picked over and empty, but the signs were still sitting on the table in front of the crumb-covered trays; Broccoli au Grande, Cauliflower Au lait, persimmon, avocado cubes. I could go on, but you catch my drift. I would have killed for a double cheeseburger or a Ballpark hot dog.

I was ready to leave anytime, but this was actually business for Heidi. She would be talking to clients or prospective clients all night long. I'd known that was the drill before we arrived. I also knew how she intended to unwind once we got home, so I just sipped the lousy beer and bided my time.

I spotted my target maybe twenty minutes later. In a room full of elegantly tailored outfits, summer silk blouses, delicate lace and sprayed on tans there she was in a gray wool skirt, with a red sweater draped over her shoulders. It looked like the perfect winter outfit for an elementary school principle. Unfortunately, it was July in Minnesota with an evening temp still hovering close to ninety and a dew point not far behind. Daft, Daphne Cochrane, Daryl Bergstrom's appointed public defender, small world.

She appeared adrift in an endless sea of chatty, head-bobbing individuals waxing eloquently about nothing while they stood in small groups all around her. She lifted a wine glass to her lips, but at just about the point where the wine approached the rim, she lowered the glass.

She appeared to be alone. Over the course of the four or five minutes I watched, she spoke to no one and no one spoke to her. If she was waiting for a friend, they were sure taking their sweet time. Not to sound too cruel, but it seemed obvious her reputation had preceded her or maybe it was just the cat hair on her sweater.

I approached with caution.

"Excuse me. Are you Ms Cochrane with the public defenders office?"

She studied me for a moment, but didn't seem to recognize me as yet another disappointed and poorly-served former client. Finally she nodded.

"I've seen you in the courtroom. How are you doing?"

"Just fine, thank you," she said crisply, but gave no follow-up question like asking my name, wondering if I practiced law, maybe sat on the bench, or was just another criminal.

"I understand you're involved in this most recent case, the one where the fellow drove the van loaded with drugs over to the parking ramp?"

She gave a slight nod and took a fake sip.

"What was his name, David something?"

"Actually, Daryl, Daryl Bergstrom."

"How is that going, do you have a trial date assigned yet?"

"No, I'm hoping we can work out a plea agreement and avoid any sort of a trial."

She'd already told me more than she should have. Based on what I'd observed, it couldn't be the wine talking, she hadn't had any. I chalked it up to ineptness.

"How does your client feel about that?"

She sighed and said, "Well, actually at this point, let's just say we're still in the initial discussion stage." She flashed a quick, cold smile. Obviously, if her innocent clients were locked up, she wouldn't have to waste her time in the court room.

"Always a pleasure chatting with you, Ms. Cochrane."

She gave a slight nod like this was an accepted fact then looked at me dismissively so I nodded and drifted back into the crowd.

Louie was right, and all my initial fears had just been confirmed, Daryl Bergstrom was royally screwed. I paid ten bucks for a glass of lousy white wine and located Heidi. She was surrounded by four paunchy guys vying for her attention. She looked grateful to see me.

"Oh, here is my significant other, Dev come here and join us. Oh, thanks," she said taking the glass of wine and handing me her empty. She took two very healthy gulps and smiled.

Two of the guys nodded and quickly left, a third stayed a half moment longer before he fled to the bar. The fourth guy hung in there for maybe five minutes talking some investment scheme that even I thought sounded shady. When he left, Heidi smiled sweetly, looked around, and said "Thanks for the rescue. He wanted to take me up to his cabin tonight."

"Can't blame him for trying. I'm ready whenever you are."

"Maybe just a while longer, I'm picking up some business."

"Like at that guy's cabin?"

"Oh, be nice. Maybe once I finish this glass of wine we'll go somewhere a little more private."

Well, there you go, Dev's already in over his head and he doesn't even know it. If you really want to help him out you can get your personal copy of Crickett from the good folks at Amazon and see what happens. Many thanks, enjoy the read, Mike Faricy.

Printed in Great Britain
by Amazon